"I'm sorry. That was wrong."

Lani blinked at him, trying to focus her fuzzy brain. "Why?"

"I'm an officer of the law. Using a position of power to take advantage of you is the very definition of sexual harassment. You have every right to be upset."

Upset? Lani wasn't the least bit upset. Russ had finally noticed her! He'd kissed her, and it had felt really, really good. She wanted him to notice her some more. "I'm not upset."

"Well, I wouldn't blame you if you added sexual harassment to that false imprisonment complaint."

"Why did you really stop?" She slid closer, until their thighs were touching and her arm brushed his. The heat of just that small contact threatened to make her go up in flames.

"I've sworn to uphold the law. There are rules." His voice was ragged and he was breathing hard.

So was she. And right this moment she didn't give a flying fig about rules.

* * *

MONTANA MAVERICKS:
What Happened at the Wedding?
A weekend Rust Creek Falls will never forget!

Dear Reader,

Brothers can be a challenge. Growing up with four of them gave me firsthand experience with this perspective. They could be obnoxious and took a ridiculous amount of pleasure from teasing their sister. Now I realize those trials and tribulation are what built character—mine. From an adult point of view I can say unequivocally that brothers are worth the trouble. Mine sure are.

A few years ago my husband had a medical crisis and was hospitalized. He's fine now but it was touch and go for a while. Questions came up—legal, medical, financial—and talking things through with men whose opinions I value so much was extraordinarily comforting during a very stressful and difficult time. My brothers listened, and that helped more than they will ever know.

In *An Officer and a Maverick*, Lani Dalton gets herself into legal *and* romantic hot water because of a promise she made to her older brother. She refuses to break her word and reveal his secret, even though it could cost her the man she loves. Russ Campbell believes in the whole truth in spite of the fact that getting it cost him everything. Working with Lani to solve the Rust Creek Falls mystery brings these two strong, stubborn, opinionated people together, but falling in love was never part of their bargain.

I loved telling Lani's story. Her conflict of loyalty resonated with me because of the close relationship I share with my own brothers. I did my best to do her story justice, and I hope you enjoy it.

Happy reading!

Teresa Southwick

An Officer and a Maverick

Teresa Southwick

HARLEQUIN® SPECIAL EDITION®

Special thanks and acknowledgment
to Teresa Southwick for her contribution to the
Montana Mavericks: What Happened at the Wedding? continuity.

ISBN-13: 978-0-373-65907-4

An Officer and a Maverick

This edition published by arrangement with Harlequin Books S.A.

For questions and comments about the quality of this book, please contact us at CustomerService@Harlequin.com.

Printed in U.S.A.

Teresa Southwick lives with her husband in Las Vegas, the city that reinvents itself every day. An avid fan of romance novels, she is delighted to be living out her dream of writing for Harlequin.

Books by Teresa Southwick

Harlequin Special Edition

The Bachelors of Blackwater Lake

A Decent Proposal
The Rancher Who Took Her In
One Night with the Boss
Finding Family...and Forever?

Montana Mavericks: 20 Years in the Saddle!

From Maverick to Daddy

Mercy Medical Montana

Her McKnight in Shining Armor
The Doctor's Dating Bargain

Montana Mavericks: Back in the Saddle

The Maverick's Christmas Homecoming

Montana Mavericks: The Texans are Coming!

Her Montana Christmas Groom

Men of Mercy Medical

The Doctor and the Single Mom
Holding Out for Doctor Perfect
To Have the Doctor's Baby
Cindy's Doctor Charming

Visit the Author Profile page at Harlequin.com for more titles.

To my brothers—Jim, Mike, Dan and Chris.
Thanks for always being there. You're my heroes.
I love you guys!

Chapter One

Fourth of July

"I wouldn't be surprised if someone strips naked and jumps in the park fountain," Lani Dalton said out loud, to no one in particular.

And no one in particular paid any attention to her, what with all the partying going on around her at the wedding reception. Everyone was having a really good time. Braden Traub had married Jennifer MacCallum, and there was little that folks in Rust Creek Falls liked more than celebrating a happy occasion. And wow, were they celebrating!

It looked as if the colors of American independence had exploded all over Rust Creek Falls Park. Picnic tables were covered by red-and white-checkered oilcloth covers, while red and blue tarps had protected people from the afternoon sun, although it had gone down a while ago. Fireworks had been shot off but people were still hanging around, dancing, talking, laughing and drinking wedding punch.

She'd just finished two-stepping with her brother and figured there was something weird going on for that to have happened. Nothing said relationship loser like dancing with your brother. Anderson was her favorite, but still… After chug-a-lugging her fourth—or was it fifth?—cup of punch, she felt a little light-headed. Sitting down suddenly seemed like an awfully good idea.

Walking around and searching for an empty seat, she wasn't watching where she was going. As a result, she ran into what felt like a brick wall and was nearly knocked onto her backside.

Strong hands reached out and steadied her. "You okay?"

Lani was pretty sure that voice belonged to Russ Campbell, a detective from Kalispell who filled in sometimes to help out Sheriff Gage Christensen here in Rust Creek Falls. She felt a familiar quiver of attraction lick through her as she looked up to confirm her suspicion. "Detective Dreamy."

"Excuse me?"

"Lani Dalton." She pointed at herself. "I work part-time at the Ace in the Hole, the local bar and grill. You're Russ Campbell."

"I know."

"I know you know who you are." She giggled and that surprised her because she wasn't normally a giggler. "I meant that *I* know who you are and was introducing myself to you. Lani Dalton," she said again.

"Okay."

"Not much of a talker, are you?"

The sheriff was short a deputy and Russ filled in at least once or twice a week. That's about how often he came into the bar but he never really paid much attention to her. She, however, had definitely noticed *him*. He was tall and broad-shouldered with thick, wavy brown hair and hazel eyes that didn't miss a thing. Except her.

He was nice-looking, but if you happened to catch a glimpse of one of his rare grins, he was absolutely adorable. As far as she knew—and she'd asked about him—no female in Rust Creek Falls or anywhere else for that matter was on the receiving end of those smiles.

"Okay, then." He cleared his throat and continually scanned the crowd of people who were getting happier by the minute. "Well, if you'll excuse me, I have to keep moving."

After months of being ignored, Lani had finally struck up a conversation. Sort of. It was an opportunity, and she wanted it to go on.

"Are you here for the bride or groom?" she asked.

"What?"

"Are you a friend of the bride or groom?"

"Neither." He indicated the gold shield hooked to the belt at the waist of his worn jeans. "I'm working. Sheriff Christensen hired me to help with crowd control."

Looking way up at him, his features seemed to blur and she swayed a little. Again, his hands reached out to steady her. She couldn't help noticing his arms, where the sleeves of his black T-shirt stretched across impressive biceps. It was swoon-worthy—that must be why she was a little woozy.

"Wow, you're really strong. And your reflexes are really good." Did she just say that? It wasn't like her to say whatever popped into her head.

He was already frowning, but her words seemed to turn the frown into a scowl. "I think you should lay off the liquor."

"All I had was punch from the reception, and they said it was some concoction with sparkling wine. No hard alcohol allowed in the public park. You should know that. So I haven't had any liquor to speak of. I swear," she said, raising her hand, palm out. "That's the thing. I work at the bar but I hardly ever drink alcohol. Am I talking too much?"

"Uh-huh." His tone was unnecessarily sarcastic. "Let's find you a place to sober up."

"I'm not drunk. And I was looking for a place to sit when you ran into me."

"For the record, *you* ran into *me*," he said.

She shook her head—that was a big mistake. "I don't think so."

"Take my word for it." His mouth tightened as he scanned the tables and didn't spot an empty place. "Let's go over here."

She felt his fingers on her arm as he led her through a maze of people who moved for him as if he was Moses parting the Red Sea. "Where are you taking me?"

"To the park fountain. The edge is wide enough to sit on, and it's cooler there."

They were passing the last of the tables when she saw her older brother Travis chatting up a pretty blonde who Lani happened to know was dating a hot-tempered, jealous cowboy. She would have warned him off, but Detective Dreamy had her in a pretty tight grip. And she spotted her other brother Anderson moving in. He would make sure Travis didn't do anything stupid.

"Here you go," Russ said after they crossed the open grassy area then reached the fountain that was spewing water in the center. "Have a seat."

Lani did and set her flag-stamped cup beside her. "Thank you, Detective."

"Yes, ma'am."

Ma'am? She was a generic female who could be anywhere from nineteen to ninety-five? Seriously? She knew he was on duty, but it wouldn't hurt him to work on his people skills. Honestly, sometimes she wondered why she was attracted to him at all. Except he was pretty cute, and she'd seen him at the bar, chatting up other people and making them laugh. Apparently, he just wasn't that into *her.* Well, she wasn't into being called *ma'am.*

"You can call me Lani. I'm not crazy about sweetie, honey or babe. But please don't ever call me ma'am. It's like nails on a chalkboard."

"Understood."

Loud voices suddenly cut through the general celebratory hum of activity. They were coming from the direction where Anderson had just walked. Skip Webster, the jealous cowboy, was arguing with Travis, who was trying to back away. Then the cowboy took a swing when Travis wasn't looking. Instead of turning the other cheek, his fists came up to retaliate. Anderson stepped between them to defuse the situation. The other man punched him, and Anderson lashed out with a fist, a knee-jerk reaction.

Skip went down then started shouting for help. He spotted Russ and hollered for an immediate arrest.

"I have to go," Russ said.

Lani had a bad feeling. "What are you going to do?"

"Arrest that guy for assault and battery."

That guy would be her brother Anderson, and that wasn't good anytime, but he had a personal legal issue pending. An arrest wouldn't work in his favor considering he was going to try to get custody of a child he'd just learned he had. Detective Russ Campbell was headed toward that ruckus unless she did something to stop him. Whatever it was had to be loud and immediate.

She heard the water gushing from the middle of the fountain behind her and did the first thing that popped into her mind, which was clearly becoming a habit tonight. She jumped into the water then gasped at the cold liquid soaking the bottom of her skirt. Russ looked at her as if she was nuts then started toward the arguing men. She couldn't think how else to stop him, so she started belting out “Firework,” her favorite Katy Perry song, which certainly made her more of a spectacle!

Well, good. Anything to help Anderson…

At the same time she smacked the water, sending a wave over the edge that hit Russ’s back. When he turned, she added some dance moves to go with the song.

He walked over and stopped in front of her. “Please come out of there, *ma’am*.”

Now she was just mad and used both hands to shower him with water. Satisfaction circled through her when he swiped a hand over his wet face, and she sang even louder. Surprisingly, she was enjoying herself.

“Okay, you’ve had your fun.” Russ was using his I’m-the-law voice. “The show here is over.”

But it seemed no one was listening to him. A few people were stopping to see what the disturbance was all about. Lani appreciated her fan club, especially because Russ kept glancing over at her brothers and Skip Webster, who was still demanding justice at the top of his lungs. Officer Campbell was clearly dying to give it to him—at the expense of her brother. She couldn’t let that happen and had to up her game.

“Come on in, the water’s fine.” She waved to the few onlookers who seemed to like the idea of a dip in the fountain.

“Whoa,” Russ said, putting his hands up to warn them off. He sent a glare in her direction. “That’s inciting public disorderliness. If you don’t come out of there voluntarily, I’m going to have to arrest you.” He glanced over his shoulder again.

Lani didn’t much like the idea of going to jail, but better her than Anderson. She didn’t have any legal problems, although that could be about to change.

“I dare you to come in and get me, Detective Dreamy.”

Russ reached out to grab her, and the frown on his face

deepened when she backed up and eluded him. "Come on, Lani. Out of the water."

"You're not the boss of me."

"As it happens, I am. I told you already, Gage brought me in for crowd control, what with the wedding and Fourth of July celebrations going on at the same time." He looked around at the happier-than-normal people scattered throughout the park. "And it was obviously the right call."

"You look hot under the collar." Although he wasn't actually wearing a collared shirt, or technically a uniform. But there was something about his ensemble of choice. The black T-shirt, jeans and boots made him about as hot as a man could get.

"Doesn't he look hot?" she said to the crowd around the fountain.

"Cool him off," someone called out.

"Okay." She sent walls of water at him as hard and fast as she could. Not much connected, though, on account of her keeping her distance so he couldn't grab her. The physical effort had her staggering, and she almost slipped.

"That does it," he said impatiently. "I'm arresting you for drunk and disorderly conduct."

"That's the nicest thing you've ever said to me, Detective." Until a few minutes ago it was practically the only thing he'd ever said with the possible exception of *could you get me a beer.*

His expression went from grim to really grim as he stepped over the edge into the fountain. Lani winced at what the water would do to those leather boots. Well, it couldn't be helped. This was for Anderson. She backed away from the advancing lawman while one person started chanting, "Lani! Lani!"

With the water choppy from their movements, it was hard to dodge him. He was bigger, stronger and faster, so she couldn't get away indefinitely. But the longer she could keep his attention focused on her, the better.

She backed up a step, and her sandal hit a slick spot on the bottom of the fountain. Down she went, not completely underwater, but enough to soak the top of her dress and ruin her hair. A second later Russ was right there in front of her, holding out a big hand to help her up. She wasn't sure where the idea came from but at this moment she didn't really care. After putting her hand in his palm, she yanked forward with all her strength. He was already off balance and fell on top of her.

"Damn it," he sputtered. "You're under arrest—"

"So you said." She brushed the hair out of her face.

He gripped her arm and tugged her up with him when he stood. "You have the right to remain silent but there's probably a snowball's chance in hell of that happening."

He finished with her rights then started walking her out of the fountain. When she slipped again, he swore under his breath before swinging her into his arms. Lani sincerely regretted that fate hadn't warned her about Russ Campbell picking her up, because she would have lost a few pounds in preparation. Points to him that he made her feel as if she weighed nothing.

After stepping out of the water, he set her down. When she wobbled a bit he asked, "Can you walk?"

"'Course. I've been doing it for years."

"Good." He curved his fingers around her upper arm and, without another word, started moving.

"Aren't you going to put the cuffs on me?" she asked sweetly.

His eyes narrowed as he looked down at her. "Are you going to resist arrest?"

"No."

"Okay, then." He kept walking and tugged her along with him.

Wow. She was going to the slammer.

For the first time since running into Russ she didn't say what popped into her head. She didn't think it would improve his mood if she started singing "Jailhouse Rock."

Russ Campbell walked Lani Dalton into the sheriff's office, his temper rising with every step. This was the last place he needed to be—and she was the last person he should be with.

Her eyes were wide, but she looked more curious than scared. "Wow, I've never been in the slammer before. This is kind of exciting."

Glancing around the room he tried to see the hub of Rust Creek Falls law enforcement through her eyes. It was a big room with a couple of desks, one where the dispatcher sat. The other was for the deputy, although Gage was short one right now. While the sheriff looked for a replacement, Russ filled in when he had time off from his detective job with the Kalispell Police Department. A room off to the right had a closing door, and that's where the sheriff worked. The place wasn't especially intimidating, but then again, he'd worked in Denver, where the department was bigger—and so were the problems.

"If you think this is cool, wait until you see the cell."

"Isn't there some law against false imprisonment?"

He took her arm and led her through a doorway, where there were two six-by-eight-foot cells. Either she was naturally sassy, putting on a front to hide her nerves, or she was still not sober enough for her situation to sink in. *Sink* wasn't the best choice of words after that surprise swim in the fountain. He couldn't believe he'd let his guard down and should have known better than to let her distract him. But Lani had been a distraction from the first time he saw her.

"This arrest is ridiculous. My father is a lawyer, and I'll be out of here before my dress dries."

He figured she was trying to look defiant but with those pretty big brown eyes of hers, she only managed to come across as innocent, and they both knew she wasn't. The drive over from the park was short, and she was still wet. He was having a devil of a time not staring at the way that bright yellow sundress clung to her small waist and curvy hips. And, dammit, the material was wet, which made it practically transparent. He didn't need her reminding him about that.

He curled his fingers around the smooth skin of her arm and tried not to think about the fact that he could use another dunking in the fountain to cool off. "Come on. I'll give you a guided tour of the slammer."

"I can see it just fine from here." She stood her ground and looked up at him, wobbling just a little. "Is it really necessary to lock me up?"

"Yes. Between the Fourth of July and that wedding reception, there's been way too much celebrating going on in this town. I've been looking the other way most of the night, but things are starting to get out of hand. My job is to not let that happen."

"So I'm the lucky one you decided to make an example of. But you don't really work here in Rust Creek Falls," she reminded him.

"That's funny. Gage Christensen pretty much said he was paying me to be on duty. Sounds like work to me." He gave her his detective glare, the one he used to intimidate people who broke the law. It came more naturally right now, since his jeans were heavy, and water squished in his boots. "Thanks to you, I'm really earning that paycheck tonight."

"The sheriff wouldn't have arrested me." Her tone was defiant. "But you're not from around here."

Not one of us, she was saying. That struck a nerve. Before he'd left the Denver Police Department everyone had been avoiding him as if he had the plague. He was treated like an outsider for blowing the whistle on a crooked cop then busted down to patrol. When his career went backward his fiancée dumped him. So much for loyalty—and love.

"I might not live in Rust Creek Falls, but I'm the one with the badge." He drilled her with a look. "You broke the law on my watch, Lani Dalton."

Her eyes widened a fraction. "Since when aren't you calling me *ma'am*?"

Not using her name was a way to keep his distance, and he'd been trying to do that since the first time he'd seen her. She had long brown hair and creamy skin that tempted a man to touch her. Resisting that temptation tested his willpower under normal circumstances, but nothing about this night was normal.

"Do you know who my father is?"

"You said he's an attorney, but right this minute I don't much care." He walked her through the doorway and into one of the cells then pulled the door shut behind them. The bolt clicked into place and echoed off the bare walls.

She flinched slightly. "So, we're locked in."

"No," he said. "You're the one locked up, and I'm the cop who has the key in his pocket."

Her eyebrow rose. "You're sure?"

"Absolutely."

"You're very confident." Lani shrugged then walked over to the metal-framed bunk. She lifted the sheet covering the thin, plastic mattress. "Wow, five-star accommodations. That looks like a yoga mat."

"Let me know if it's comfortable. You're going to be here awhile." She wasn't as far gone as some he'd seen under the influence. In his opinion, she could be left alone, and that was a good thing. Russ didn't have time to babysit the princess. "It's nuts out there, and your stunt in the fountain took me away from where I need to be."

"Lighten up, Detective. Everyone's just having fun."

"I don't think the cowboy who got decked was having such a great time."

"Oh? I didn't notice." She put just a little too much innocence in those words.

"Then you're the only one in Rust Creek Falls who didn't. Now I have to go deal with the guy who decked him."

"You're not really going to arrest him?" Her bravado slipped for the first time since he'd politely suggested she exit the public fountain.

"Yeah, I am. On the upside, you'll have some company in here tonight."

"Seriously, you're going to leave me alone?"

Apparently, the reality of the situation was sinking in, because some of the spunk finally seemed to drain out of her.

"You'll be fine."

"I don't think so." She put a shaking hand up to her forehead and swayed on her feet, the color draining from her face. "I'm feeling a little dizzy. I think I might be sick."

In one stride he was beside her, sliding an arm around her waist. She collapsed against him, clingier than the wet dress. She was deadweight, and her hand clutched him, just below his belt, trying to hang on and keep from falling. He practically carried her to the bunk and settled her on it, sitting beside her.

"Take deep breaths. Put your head between your knees."

"I'll fall on my face." She sat stiffly on the thin, plastic mattress, hands clenched into fists on either side of her, and breathed deeply several times. "I think I'm feeling a little better."

Russ studied her face and noted the color was returning. "I'll get you some water."

"No." That was a little more emphatic than necessary. "What I mean is, I'm afraid it might come back up."

"After drinking too much, the best thing you can do is hydrate. And a couple of aspirin wouldn't hurt, either."

There was something about her that brought out his protective streak, but he chalked it up to doing his duty. The job he could handle, but being in this small space with Lani Dalton was trouble. There wasn't enough room for him to avoid the sweet scent of her skin. That made him want to lean in even closer and find out if that sassy, sarcastic mouth of hers would taste as good as he'd been imagining for months now.

Abruptly, he stood and turned his back on her.

"Is something wrong?" she asked.

Behind him there was the sound of the plastic mattress creaking as she shifted her weight. He turned, and the innocent expression he'd noted moments ago was back in place. She sat quietly looking at him, hands folded in her lap. Her dress was still wet, and the sight of the thin cotton clinging to her breasts ignited the familiar conflict inside him.

He was really attracted to her but knew that acting on it was a complication he just didn't need. Not now, not ever. His heart had taken a hit, through and through, and that experience made him determined not to be a fool again. His new philosophy was never trust anyone unless they gave you a reason to. So he'd decided not to get to know Lani Dalton better. And she'd done nothing tonight to make him regret the decision. Although that wet dress was giving his self-control a real workout.

"Okay, I have to go now. Looks like you're fine."

"I still feel nauseous. What if I have to throw up?"

"Do what you have to do." And he would do the same,

which meant getting out of here, away from her. "And right now I have to go make rounds and investigate that assault-and-battery incident. I'll be back before you even know I'm gone."

"Solitary will be an improvement." She folded her arms over her chest, trying to look bored.

"Be sure to put that on the customer satisfaction survey."

But Russ was sure some vulnerability was trickling out. And with that thought he knew it was past time to get the hell away from her. He moved the short distance to the barred door at the same time feeling his jeans pocket for the key. The familiar outline of the metal wasn't in the usual place so he dug deeper. It wasn't there. He checked his left pocket then the back ones.

Nothing.

"That's the damnedest thing."

"Is there a problem?" She didn't sound the least bit anxious.

"I don't have the key." He met her gaze, waiting for her to mock this turn of events.

Lani held her breath, waiting for Russ to figure out that she'd taken his keys and shoved them under the "yoga mat." She was feeling very bold for some reason and figured she had nothing to lose. The plan was conceived in desperation, and she didn't expect to get away with it, but couldn't think of any other way to stop him from arresting her brother.

"I guess you forgot to put the keys in your pocket. And that's understandable considering how crazy it is out there. It feels like a horror movie—night of the living party-animal apocalypse."

One corner of his mouth tilted up, and for a moment she thought he was going to give her one of his adorable smiles. But he seemed to catch himself then pulled his cell phone from a back pocket.

"I'll just give Gage a call." He pushed some keys and frowned. "Apparently, water and sensitive electronic devices are incompatible."

"I'm so sorry." And she really was. Ruining his phone hadn't crossed her mind when all she could think about was helping her brother. And the longer Russ was distracted with her, the better it would be for Anderson. So she was kind of glad he couldn't call the sheriff. "I'll pay for a new phone," she offered.

He glared at her. "I don't suppose you have one that works."

"I do. Because it's at home."

"A likely story."

"Seriously?" She glanced down at her dress and realized the still-damp cotton made her body half a step from being naked. She should be embarrassed, but that tendency toward boldness was still firing on all cylinders. "I rode to the park with my parents and left my purse at home. And really, if I had one on me, it would be as wet as yours. It would also have to be somewhere a gentleman wouldn't go looking for it."

"No one would accuse me of being a gentleman, but you're right about one thing. There's no point in searching even if you're lying."

"Well, that hurts my feelings."

"Which part?" he asked.

That she was a liar? Or her body was not interesting enough? "Both."

But what was that saying about poking an angry bear? Lani had lost count of all the times Russ Campbell had been at the Ace in the Hole with Gage Christensen and never talked to her. She'd asked Gage about him and knew Russ was a detective on the Kalispell Police Department and had moved back to Montana from Denver. No one knew why.

Now she was finally having a conversation with him, but it was about her being deceptive and lacking even a speck of sex appeal. That was disappointing and humiliating in equal parts. And, if that wasn't bad enough, now there was every reason to believe he really didn't like her. Well, he was pretty cute, but that didn't stop her from being a little annoyed with him right now, too.

He sighed. "I just meant that if you had a phone, yours wouldn't work, either."

"It's really not important," she finally said.

That all-seeing hazel gaze of his narrowed on her. "You're one cool customer, Lani Dalton."

"Oh?" Cool as in attractive, intriguing and alluring? Or cool as in nervy and annoying?

"Yeah. I've seen women fall apart over being stopped for a speeding ticket, and you don't seem the least bit upset about the fact that you've been arrested and locked up in jail."

"So are you," she reminded him.

"But I'm not in legal trouble."

Okay, he won that round. She wasn't too worried about the fountain dance, although after tonight probably a notice would be posted on it with a warning to keep out. But destroying his phone and helping herself to the jail cell keys could be a problem. Intellectually, she knew that, but her lovely buzz made it impossible to care.

"I'm not really worried. Ben Dalton is my father. You may have heard he has an excellent legal reputation."

"Ah." He nodded, but the tone and his expression hinted at a deep well of sarcasm.

"What does that mean?"

"That you're the little princess. Rules don't apply to you because daddy can find a loophole and make it all go away." He moved back until bumping up against the bars stopped him.

Lani was pretty sure he was staying as far away from her as he could get, and it bummed her more than a little.

"You don't know my father. Or me." She didn't much care about the angry defensiveness in her tone. Russ had gone out of his way *not* to know her. "He took an oath to uphold the law and wouldn't compromise his principles. Ever. Not even for one of his children."

That was the truth and probably why Anderson hadn't said anything to anyone else in the family about his legal trouble and made her swear not to, either. She'd caught her brother at a weak moment, and he apparently had been feeling the stress of carrying this burden alone. That's the only reason she knew.

Russ didn't say anything, but clearly he wasn't a happy camper. And who could blame him? Her cotton dress was drying faster than his jeans and T-shirt, and those boots were probably dead to him. She should offer to pay for those, too.

"Look, Russ—"

"I should be out there. Gage hired me to help him keep the peace with so much going on today, and now he's alone." He started pacing. "There's no telling when he'll check in. It might not be until morning what with half the town three sheets to the wind."

Guilt weighed on Lani. If only she knew that Anderson and Travis had walked away and not escalated the situation, she would confess her sins and take her punishment. But she didn't know and had to keep up her distraction as long as possible.

"Okay," she said, "we're stuck. When life gives you lemons, make lemonade. We should talk."

The look he sent in her direction was ironic. "I suppose it was too much to hope we wouldn't have to."

"Are you always this mean or do I just bring out the

worst in you?" She met his gaze and refused to look away. "We should get to know each other."

"That's really not a good idea—"

"It could be. You have an opinion of me. I have an opinion of you and maybe we're both wrong. Attitude is everything. Think of it as an opportunity to make a better impression." She refused to be put off by the stubborn, skeptical expression on his face. "Okay, I'll start."

Chapter Two

Russ stared long and hard at his prisoner. She was sitting on the bunk in a jail cell looking all wide-eyed and perky and pretty damned appealing. If she was the least bit intimidated by him or the situation, he couldn't see it. Although as she'd so helpfully pointed out, he was locked in, too, which kind of took the starch out of his intimidation factor.

How the hell could he have forgotten to put the keys in his pocket before walking her in here? That wasn't like him. The movement was automatic, muscle memory.

As much as he hated to admit it, she was probably right. It *had* been a crazy night, and there'd been a lot of calls to the sheriff's office. He'd been busy, distracted.

Now he was uncomfortably and undeniably distracted by his "roomie," who wanted to share personal information. Last time he'd checked, it wasn't a cop's job to spill his guts to a detainee.

"You want to join hands and sing 'Kumbaya' because

it's not bad enough that we're locked up together?" he asked.

"No." She shifted on the bunk and spread out the damp skirt of her sundress. "Look, the fact is that we're stuck in here, unless one of us can bend steel in their bare hands, and that sure isn't me."

"Superman. That's just great." He nodded grimly.

Doing the right thing had cost Russ his law enforcement career in Denver, but somehow that never seemed to happen to the legendary comic book superhero. And Lois Lane never dumped him when everyone else thought he was gum on the bottom of their shoe.

"Seriously, Russ, we don't know how long it might be before someone comes looking."

"I don't think it will be that long before Gage checks in." He hoped he was right about that, but the situation in the park hadn't been quieting down when he'd brought Lani in.

"That's just wishful thinking because obviously you don't like me very much."

"Arresting you wasn't personal." Russ figured it was best not to put a finer point on that statement by saying he didn't *want* to like her. There was a difference. "It's my job."

"Whatever." She met his gaze. "We could sit here in awkward silence. Or we can make conversation to help the time pass a little faster."

He hated to admit it, but she had a point. "Okay. But if you say anything about braiding each other's hair, I'm pretty sure my head will explode."

"If only." She gathered the stringy, drying strands of her long hair and lifted them off her neck. "I'd give anything to be able to brush this mess."

"You should have thought of that before dancing in the fountain—"

She held up a finger to stop his words. "I thought we had a truce."

"My bad."

"Okay, then. Have a seat." She patted the mattress next to her. "There's nowhere else to sit in here. I'll have to have a word with your decorator about what a conversation area should look like."

He didn't want to sit next to her but couldn't say so or he'd have to explain why. And he didn't quite understand that himself, other than the fact that he'd just arrested her. Since she occupied the center of the bunk and showed no inclination to move, he took the end, as far away from her as he could get.

Lani looked at him expectantly and when he didn't say anything, she cleared her throat. "I was born here in Rust Creek Falls twenty-six years ago, number five of six children."

"Braiding hair is starting to sound like a high-speed freeway pursuit." When she laughed, the merry sound burrowed inside him, landing like a gentle rain that softened rock-hard soil.

"Compared to what you do my life *is* boring, but I like it. And I love this town." She shrugged. "I live with my parents here in Rust Creek Falls and work on the family ranch, which is north of town. I do everything from mucking out stalls to riding fence and feeding stock."

"What about working at the Ace in the Hole?"

"That's part-time. Rosey Traven, the owner, is the best boss in the world."

Russ had been in his share of bars and seen how badly guys who drank too much behaved. A woman as beautiful as Lani would be a first-class target for come-ons and drunken passes. The thought of some jerk hitting on her made him almost as mad as the water in his boots. But all he said was, "It probably gets rough in there."

"It can sometimes. But Rosey's husband, Sam, was a

navy SEAL. He knows three hundred ways to immobilize a creep with a cocktail napkin."

That made Russ feel a little better, but not much. "What do you like about the job?"

Her shrug did mind-blowing things to what was under the top part of that sundress. The material was thin, still damp, and he could almost see her breasts. They looked just about perfect to him and made his hands ache to touch her and find out for sure. And this wasn't the first time he'd experienced that particular feeling around her, but he'd always made sure not to get too close.

"I'm a people person," she finally said. "I like chatting with the regulars, and almost everyone in Rust Creek Falls comes in to hang out at some point or other. You know, guys' nights, girls' night out, poker games…or people just coming in for a burger and a beer. I like hearing what's going on in their lives and apparently, that makes them want to talk to me."

He laughed, but there was no humor in the sound.

"What's funny?" she asked, a small frown marring the smooth skin of her forehead.

"My job is the polar opposite. I'm a detective for Kalispell PD, and no one wants to talk to me."

"I see what you mean." She smiled her happy, under-the-influence smile. "But can you blame them? It makes a difference when your job is selling drinks as opposed to interrogating a perp."

"I suppose."

She half turned toward him in her earnestness to make him understand. "I'm somewhere between a family counselor and confessor. People feel comfortable baring their heart and soul to me, and I take that as an obligation. I consider it part of my job description to offer sensible advice or sometimes to simply listen. Whatever the situation calls for."

"I had no idea the job was so demanding."

"Go ahead. Make fun." There was annoyance in the look she settled on him. "But I think people trust me."

"In what way?"

"Rust Creek Falls is a small town. Everyone knows everyone, and some people think that gives them the right to every last detail of a person's life. But some things shouldn't be spread around. I know the difference, and folks who know me know I'll keep that sort of information to myself."

"I know what you mean about a small town," he said.

"How? Kalispell is a pretty big city compared to Rust Creek."

"I grew up in Boulder Junction. It's a small town about halfway between here and Kalispell."

She nodded. "I know it. That's farming country, right?"

"Yeah. My family has one. Mainly they grow wheat, corn and hay. But they have smaller crops, too."

"Like what?"

"Apples. Potatoes. Barley."

"Sounds like a pretty big farm."

"Yeah." One of the biggest in Montana.

"Family, huh? Does that mean you weren't found under an arugula leaf?"

"It does." The corners of his mouth turned up a little in spite of his resolve to keep his distance. "I actually have parents and siblings."

"Plural?" she asked. "Boys? Girls?"

"Two brothers and a sister. I'm the oldest." He didn't usually talk this much, but there was something about Lani Dalton, something in her eyes that said she was sincerely interested. She was listening, and he didn't even have to buy a drink, just arrest her for drinking too much.

"So you grew up in a small town, too. Have you done any traveling?" she asked.

"Some."

"Lucky you. I've never really been anywhere." There was a wistful expression in her eyes. "Have you ever thought about leaving Montana?"

"No." Not since he'd come back from Colorado a couple years ago.

"Really?"

Russ had done enough interrogations to spot a technique for coaxing information out of someone who was reluctant to part with it. He wasn't inclined to do that. "Really."

She studied him for several moments then nodded, as if she knew the subject was closed. "Tell me about your brothers and sister. Anyone married? Do you have any nieces or nephews?"

"No to all of the above. What about you?"

"I have two sisters and three brothers. The oldest two were at Braden and Jennifer's wedding—"

"What?" he asked when she stopped talking.

"Nothing." But her body language changed. She sat up straighter and shook her head. There was something she didn't want to talk about. "My brother Caleb got married last year. My sister Paige took the plunge the year before that, and now she and her husband have a baby boy."

"Good for them."

"Yeah, they seem happy. But I'm not sure it would work for me."

On a night full of surprises, that might have been the biggest one yet. "Doesn't every girl dream of a long white dress and walking down the aisle?"

She laughed. "I'm not every girl. And in case you didn't get the memo, a woman doesn't need a man to be happy and fulfilled."

"Spoken like a woman who's been dumped." He was watching her and saw a slight tightening of her full lips, indicating he'd gotten that one right.

Irritated, she leaned in closer to make a point. "Is that observation based on crack investigative skill, Detective Campbell?"

"Nope. It's based more on gut instinct."

"Wow, who knew I was going to get locked up with Dr. Phil?"

"I have my moments." He could feel the heat from her body and her breath on his cheek. The sensations were taking him to a place he was trying very hard not to go. "You know, Lani, it's none of my business, but I don't think you should let one bad experience sour you on marriage."

"Why? Because you're married and highly recommend it?"

"No."

"Ever been married?"

"No."

"Then how are you qualified to endorse marriage?"

"There's a lot to be said for it." He hoped that didn't sound as lame as he thought, especially because it didn't really answer the question. He just kind of liked the way her eyes flashed when she was annoyed. It made the green and gold flecks stand out, warm colors that hinted at the fire inside.

"Like what?" she demanded.

"Well..." He thought for several moments. "Having someone waiting for you at the end of the day." He'd missed that when Alexis walked out on him. "Someone there to listen to you bellyache about the bad stuff. And celebrate the good."

"I have girlfriends for that." She slid a little closer, practically quivering with indignation. "Frankly, I don't get the appeal of being with one person for the rest of your life. Guys just stand you up. Make promises they don't intend to keep. I mean, seriously? The very expression—tying the knot. Sounds an awful lot like a noose around your neck."

"You said yourself that marriage is working for your brother and sister," he challenged.

"Yeah, well, those two always were the black sheep of the family. Who wants to be tied down? Take the plunge? Think about that. Every expression referring to wedded bliss has a negative connotation. And I don't think I'd like having to answer to someone else when I want to come and go."

If that's what she wanted, why should it bother him? And that, in a nutshell, was the damn problem. It did bother him. The idea of her playing the field seemed wrong. When confronted with right and wrong, wrong tweaked his temper every time.

"You know what?" he said. "Forget I mentioned it."

She rolled her eyes. "How come your badge is all bent out of shape? You brought it up."

"No, you did," he reminded her. "Asking about my family and telling me about yours."

"I thought most guys wanted to be bachelors, but you're the one pushing the perks of matrimony. I disagree with everything you said, and now you're crabby—" She stopped. "Make that *more* crabby."

She was full of intensity and obviously capable of strong feelings. More than his next breath he wanted to hold all that passion in his arms. And every rational part of his brain not drenched in testosterone was telling him to move as far away from her as he could get. The problem was the locked door meant he couldn't go anywhere. Shutting down this conversation was his only choice.

"You are absolutely right. Being on my own is good. I like being on my own." His face was only inches from hers. "The best thing about my life is not having any commitments."

"A girl could get a serious case of whiplash the way you

change your mind. Just what makes you so happy about not being committed?"

Before Russ even knew what was happening, he closed the small distance between them. "Because if I were committed, I couldn't do this."

He hadn't planned to kiss her, didn't know he was going to until his lips touched hers. But once it happened, he couldn't seem to stop. She had, without a doubt, the sweetest mouth he'd ever tasted. He cupped her smooth, soft cheek in his hand, ready to go wherever she would take him. Her sigh of contentment said she'd take him somewhere special, make him forget where they were.

That thought was like getting a bucket of ice water dumped over his head. They were in jail, dammit. With an effort, he pulled back and dropped his hand. "I'm sorry. That was wrong."

Lani blinked at him, trying to focus her fuzzy brain. "Why?"

"I'm an officer of the law. Using a position of power to take advantage of you is the very definition of sexual harassment. You have every right to be upset."

Upset? Lani wasn't the least bit upset. He'd finally noticed her! He'd kissed her and it felt really, really good. She wanted him to notice her some more. "I'm not upset."

"Well, I wouldn't blame you if you added sexual harassment to that false imprisonment complaint."

"Why did you really stop?" She slid closer, until their thighs were touching, and her arm brushed his. The heat of just that small contact threatened to make her go up in flames.

"I've sworn to uphold the law. There are rules." His voice was ragged, and he was breathing hard.

So was she. And right this moment she didn't give a flying fig about rules.

"Maybe rules were made to be broken." She searched his eyes for a moment and then leaned in and kissed him.

She felt his hesitation and heard him make a sound that was somewhere between a groan and a curse. Suddenly, he was kissing her back, touching her everywhere, and she was tugging the shirt from his waistband. All she could think about was getting closer. The sound of their ragged breathing filled the small space.

"Damn it. I don't have protection." Frustration snapped in his voice.

"It's okay," she whispered. "I'm on the pill."

"Oh, thank God."

He slid her dress up to her waist then yanked his shirt off and lowered his jeans. She couldn't believe that he wanted her as much as she did him. Still, it seemed they'd been heading toward this since the moment he'd scooped her into his arms earlier. Never taking his mouth from hers, he gently lowered her to the mattress and slid her panties off. He ran his hand down her side, letting his fingers graze her breast. Everywhere he touched she caught fire, but it wasn't nearly enough.

"Lani, I want you." The words were hardly more than a breath against her lips.

All she could say was yes and that was all he needed to hear. When he tenderly and carefully entered her, she wrapped her legs around his waist. With every stroke he took her higher until pleasure exploded through her and she cried out from the sheer power of the feelings.

"Lani—" A groan cut off his words, and he went still then found his own release.

Their breathing slowed and returned to normal, the only sound in the small cell. Cuddled up to Russ, being held in his strong arms, made Lani decide that getting arrested wasn't so bad, after all. She wasn't sure what she'd been drinking at the wedding reception, but something had lowered her inhibitions and let her go for it.

And suddenly she was really sleepy and found her eyes sliding shut.

She wasn't sure how long she dozed, but sometime later she felt him move.

"My arm is numb."

Lani blinked her eyes open at the sound of the deep voice. It took her several moments to realize where she was. And what she'd done. What *they'd* done, right here in the cell. And he'd let her sleep, long enough for his arm to go numb. That was awfully sweet.

"We better get dressed." Without waiting for a response, Russ rolled away from her and off the bunk. He picked up her panties and handed them to her. Then turned his back while she righted her clothes.

"Thanks." Although he was correct that they should dress, she missed the warmth of his arms around her, his body pressed to hers. And he'd gone back to the good-looking guy who didn't notice her.

A little while ago they'd been as intimate as a man and woman could be, but now he wouldn't even look at her, and you could cut the awkwardness with a dull knife. She straightened her dress then stared at the bars. If they weren't locked in, she could quietly slip away, but any walk of shame was limited to a six-by-eight-foot cell.

"I feel as if I should say that this isn't something I normally do." Russ met her gaze.

"Me, either."

"Are you okay?" he asked. "You look kind of—I don't know." His mouth thinned to a straight line, clearly regretting what happened. "I'm sorry."

"Don't be." She shook her head. An apology implied what they'd done was wrong, and she refused to believe that. The responsibility for them being in this situation was hers, and she had to confess. "Look, I need to tell you something—"

He held up his hand to stop her. "I know what you're going to say. I guess technically it's morning and you hate yourself."

"No, I—"

The outer door opened and slammed closed. "Russ? You in here?"

"Back here," he called. There was a grim look on his face. Probably because he was about to face his boss and explain how he got locked in here.

Gage appeared in the doorway and did a double take when he saw them in the cell. "What the hell?"

"Boy, am I glad to see you." Russ dragged his fingers through his hair.

"You want to explain to me what's going on here?" the sheriff asked.

"Not really. But I guess you should know, since you're the boss." Russ took a deep breath. "I lost the key."

A wry look settled on Gage's face. "I'm not a detective like you, but I sort of figured that out. It's the part where you're in the cell with Lani Dalton that could use some kind of explanation."

"I arrested her for creating a public disturbance."

"It's true," said Lani, looking as apologetic as possible—and truthfully, she felt pretty bad at the moment. At least, about nearly getting caught doing the deed with Russ. She'd only meant to stop him from arresting her brother, not get him in trouble altogether! "I was dancing in the park fountain. And I pulled him in. I swear I didn't have liquor. Not really. They'd said that punch was only sparkling wine, but *punch* was sure the right word for the wallop it gave me—"

"This is my responsibility—" Russ's voice was clipped.

She felt the least she could do was come to his defense,

since this was all her fault. But he gave her a don't-do-me-any-favors glare that kept her silent.

"Be that as it may," Gage said, "Russ, I'd like to know why you were on that side of the barred door when it automatically closed."

"Lani—the prisoner—was anxious about being left alone. And argumentative."

"You couldn't have calmed her down and argued with her while standing over here?" Shaking his head, Gage put a hand on the barred door in question. "Rookie mistake."

"How long before I live this down?" Russ asked.

"Hard to say. Could take on legend status," the sheriff told him, grinning. He inserted the key, and the lock opened with a loud click. "Good thing I have another set of keys or you'd be stuck in there a whole lot longer."

Lani was okay with that, but one look at Russ told her that one minute more than necessary in here with her was about as appealing as brain surgery with a chain saw. When the door slid wide, Russ walked out and Lani started to follow him. He stopped, and she ran into his broad back.

"Not so fast." He turned and looked down at her. "In case it slipped your mind, I arrested you."

It kind of *had* slipped her mind, what with having sex in the slammer. She may have locked them in, but he'd started *that.* All things considered, the park incident felt like years instead of hours ago, and her head was starting to pound.

"Let her go, Russ." Gage rested his hands on his hips. "Given the way this night has gone, her behavior is small potatoes. Sometimes you can pick and choose which hill to die on, and this is one of those times. She's not a hardened criminal, and it was nothing more than mischief. You and I have more important things to deal with right now."

Russ looked at the sheriff for several moments then nodded. "Whatever you say."

"Do you need a ride home, Lani?" Gage asked.

"No." She was already feeling guilty for taking up law enforcement time on false pretenses.

"Okay, then. Don't get into any more trouble and make me regret cutting you some slack." Gage gave her the intimidating lawman look that was becoming familiar tonight.

She saluted. "Yes, sir."

Gage grinned again then turned and walked out, leaving them alone on the free side of the cell door. Lani was feeling equally happy to be sprung and guilty for what she'd done. Even though protecting her brother was a sound enough reason as far as she was concerned. But all of a sudden it seemed very important that Russ not think too badly of her.

She cleared her throat. "Russ, I just want to say—"

"Not now, Lani. I've got work to do. And first I have to make sure you get home okay."

He walked her to the door of the sheriff's office then opened it and waited for her to go outside. When she did, he let the automatic locking door close behind them then moved to the sheriff's cruiser parked at the curb and opened the rear door. She had no choice but to get in.

Shouldn't she feel better about this reprieve? About this get-out-of-jail-free card? She probably would except that she felt guilty, and Russ refused to even look at her.

So nothing had changed. He was back to ignoring her.

Chapter Three

When Russ pulled the sheriff's department cruiser to a stop in front of her house, Lani opened the rear door. It was a short ride from the office, but he hadn't said a word to her the whole time. The overhead light revealed the tension tightening his jaw.

"Can you get inside by yourself?" he asked.

She almost winced at the curt, cold tone. "Of course. Why wouldn't I?"

"There might not be anyone home. You don't have a purse and that means no keys."

Guilt swept through her, and she wished for another cup of wedding reception punch and whatever magical ingredient had made her bold and fearless. She didn't feel that way now.

"I can get in. Thanks." She met his gaze. "Look, Russ, let me just say—"

"Please close the door, Lani."

"Okay. I'm sorry. Good night." Empty words because

she knew his night had already been anything but good. Thanks to her. But the next time she saw him at the Ace in the Hole, she would buy him a beer and not let him ignore her. "I appreciate you bringing me home."

She got out, shut the cruiser door then watched until the red taillights disappeared when he turned the corner. One glance at the house's dark windows told her that her parents and sister were in bed, which was a big relief. There might just be a chance that her fountain performance would slide by under the Dalton family radar.

Her parents kept an emergency house key hidden in the backyard under one of the bricks that lined the patio. She retrieved it and let herself in the French door to the family room. Moving quietly through the shadowy interior toward the kitchen, she saw the microwave's green digital readout of the time. Holy cow, how did it get to be so late?

Apparently, time really did fly when one was having fun. And she really had been—between the time she'd gotten Russ talking about himself and the moment he'd frozen her out after making love to her. Probably she should feel remorse about being "easy" but couldn't muster it. What happened had really meant something to her but now, thinking about being in his arms, the experience seemed surreal, as if she'd been dreaming.

It was good she wouldn't have to face her family right now. She'd have time for her head to clear and sort out what went down before seeing anyone.

Suddenly, she heard the click of a light switch and lights blazed on.

"Where in the world have you been?" Her sister, Lindsay, was standing at the bottom of the stairs where the kitchen, family room and front hall all came together.

Startled, Lani let out a screech. "Dear God, you scared the crap out of me."

"Sorry." Her sister didn't sound sorry. She sounded

irritated and anxious. "I heard noises and came down to check it out."

"Why are you still up?"

"Couldn't sleep. I was worried. In the park I looked everywhere for you. We were supposed to meet after the fireworks and come home together."

"Unless one of us hooked up, remember?" When they'd discussed the plan, Lani had added that but was joking. She wasn't psychic and never in the world could have predicted she would hook up with Russ.

"I guess that means you were with a guy?" Lindsay's brown hair was pulled into a messy ponytail on top of her head. She was wearing boxer-style sleep shorts with SpongeBob SquarePants printed on them and a pink, spaghetti-strapped tank top.

"Define *with*," Lani hedged.

"Look, I saw you get out of the sheriff's car just now. Why did he drive you home? Something is up, and I want to know what it is."

Her sister's voice was a little louder, and Lani glanced at the stairs leading to the second floor, where her parents were sleeping. "Shh. You'll wake Mom and Dad."

"I'm okay with that." Lindsay folded her arms over her chest. "What in the world has gotten into everyone tonight? You disappeared. Travis and Anderson got into it with Skip Webster in the park—"

After what happened with Russ in jail, Lani had forgotten about her brother. "Is he okay?"

"Skip is fine. He has a fat lip, but with that temper of his it's not the first time."

"Not Skip! Anderson. And Travis," she added.

"The boys are fine. Upstairs sleeping it off. Anderson had too much to drink to drive himself back to his place and bunked in his old room for the night. But it's not like them to drink that much." Lindsay gave her an accusing look. “I could have used your help. Where were you? Are you okay? And why did the sheriff bring you home?”

“Technically it wasn’t the sheriff,” she said cautiously.

“That’s not the point.” But then she said, “So who was it?”

“Russ Campbell.”

“Who?”

“I’ve told you about him. The detective from Kalispell PD who comes in to the Ace in the Hole.” *And acts as if* I’m *invisible*, she thought.

Lindsay looked puzzled for a moment, then the confusion cleared. “Yeah. The really cute cop who doesn’t know you’re alive?”

He does now, Lani thought. After what they did, he would have a hard time ignoring her from now on. But she only said, “That’s the one. He was working a shift for Gage Christensen because of the holiday and wedding reception in the park.”

“Smart,” Lindsay said. “It was crazy out there. I still can’t believe I had the guts to get between our brothers and Skip Webster. It’s weird. And all I had to drink was the punch from the reception.”

“Weird, all right,” Lani agreed.

“And you still haven’t explained where *you* were tonight.”

“Oh, you know—”

“Not really. And that’s why I’m asking.” Lindsay’s blue eyes narrowed.

Lani wasn’t up for this. “Look, just because you’re in law school and working in Dad’s office this summer doesn’t mean you can cross-examine me.”

“And just because I’m the baby of the family doesn’t mean I’m not entitled to know what’s going on. If you won’t tell me where you were, I’m sure Dad can get it out of you. We both know how good he is.”

Her sister half turned, as if to head upstairs and make

good on her threat. "Wait," Lani said. "Don't wake him. It's late."

"Okay, then, spill."

She took a deep breath and said, "I was arrested."

"What?"

"I was dancing in the park fountain. Singing, too. When Russ Campbell tried to pull me out, I pulled him in." Lani shrugged. "I forced him to take me to jail."

"Why would you do that?" Lindsay blinked, completely at a loss.

"Seemed like a good way to keep Detective Campbell from arresting Anderson for assault and battery."

"So you took one for Team Dalton?" The younger sister shook her head. "That fight was no big deal."

"But Skip Webster was demanding someone be arrested, and Russ seemed more than happy to oblige."

"But there was no real harm done. Surely Dad would have gotten Anderson out of jail and smoothed it over."

"I figured it would go easier for me. Being a woman. And being a public nuisance is less serious than punching someone."

"You do realize," Lindsay started, "that Dad would say you should have let our intoxicated brothers suffer the consequences of their actions?"

That sounded about right for Ben Dalton, Lani thought. But she couldn't reveal the real reason it was necessary to keep Anderson's record spotless. When their brother was ready, he would tell the rest of the family.

"At the time, it seemed like a good idea to keep Russ distracted."

"Russ? Sounds like you got pretty chummy with him in the clink." Lindsay stared her down. "You're not saying anything, and I know that look on your face."

"I don't know what you mean." She knew exactly what

her sister meant. They were close enough that the sisters knew if one wasn't telling the whole truth.

"Then I'll put a finer point on it." Lindsay moved closer. "You just said you had to keep Russ distracted. That sounds premeditated to me. And you're on a first-name basis with him. Just what did you do to keep him distracted?"

Lani felt heat creep up her neck and settle in her cheeks. If only she could have put a bag over her head.

Lindsay's eyes grew wide even though Lani hadn't said a word. "You didn't."

"Of course I didn't sleep with him."

"I didn't *say* you slept with him. What makes you think that's what I meant? Why is that the first thing that popped into your head?"

"Good gravy, Lindsay." Lani had no doubt her sister would be a very good lawyer someday. "You sound like a prosecutor."

"I'll take that as a compliment." There was a pleased expression on her pretty face just before her eyes narrowed. "But I'm not stupid, sis. Something happened between you and Russ. You were gone for hours, and I'd like an explanation."

"It's not a big deal." Liar, she thought. She would throw her sister a bone and get her off that line of questioning. "We were in the locked cell together. I managed to take his keys and hide them. And before you start, I didn't want him to dump me there just so he could go back to the park and arrest Anderson."

"This just gets better and better." Lindsay shook her head. "I'm speechless."

"That's a first."

"How did you finally get out?"

"Gage came looking for Russ. He let us out. When Russ wanted to keep me in jail, the sheriff talked him out of it and said there were bigger problems to deal with."

"That's true," her sister said. "But I can't believe how underhanded you are."

"You say underhanded, I say resourceful. The good news is that Anderson is in the clear."

Lindsay met her gaze. "You're the one I'm worried about. He didn't get arrested. I hope Russ doesn't change his mind and press charges."

Lani hoped so, too.

When her alarm clock went off at zero-dark-thirty, Lani felt as if she'd just closed her eyes. But the holiday was over and she had to work at the ranch today. The cows and horses still got hungry and needed attention even if their humans got only a couple hours of sleep. As motivational speeches went it wasn't great, but she didn't have the energy to kick herself in the ass.

She dragged on jeans, shirt and boots. Pulled her hair into a ponytail, brushed her teeth, washed her face and put on sunscreen. On her way downstairs she smelled coffee, and her attitude perked up a little, no pun intended. No one in this house but her was ever up this early and brewed coffee, so there must be a God.

She walked into the kitchen and saw Anderson grabbing the bottle of Tylenol from the cupboard above the coffeepot. She was happy that he was here and not in a jail cell.

"Can I have a couple of those, too?" she asked.

He held out the bottle. "You look terrible."

"Thanks. So do you." Lani shook some of the white caplets into her palm. "I feel as if there are teeny, tiny elves hammering a Sousa march on the inside of my skull."

"Me, too." He poured coffee into a mug and held it out. "Can you give me a ride to my truck? It's at the park."

"Sure. How did you get home last night?"

"I'm not exactly sure." He dragged his fingers through his brown hair. "It's all a blur. And I don't even know why.

I feel hungover, but all I had to drink was that punch at Braden and Jennifer's wedding reception."

She blew on her coffee. "So you don't remember giving Skip Webster a fat lip?"

There was a frown in his blue eyes as he flexed the fingers on his right hand. "Yeah, that would explain the bruised knuckles, but it's all a blur."

"Hitting someone isn't your style at all, Anderson." She'd always looked up to her brother and knew what a good man he was. He's the one who told her Jase Harvey was a sweet-talking charmer who would crush her heart then held her while she cried when he turned out to be right. If only she'd listened to him.

"Dad raised us boys to never start a fight. But he always said that if anyone else did, don't run away from it." He rubbed a calloused thumb over the thick handle of his mug.

"If it's any consolation, I saw what happened. Skip swung at Travis when he wasn't looking, and you stepped in. He hit you first."

"Okay, then." He nodded grimly and met her gaze. "If you were a spectator to that, I guess that means you stayed out of trouble."

"Define *trouble*."

Those big-brother blue eyes of his zeroed in on her. "What happened, Lani?"

She figured he had a right to know and was the only person she could tell the whole truth. "Russ Campbell was going to arrest you for assault and battery on Skip Webster, so I created a diversion."

"What did you do?"

"It was hot." She had been feeling no fear and wasn't sure why. And just before the incident she'd thought about someone jumping into the fountain but hadn't expected that person to be her. "I took a dip in the park fountain, and there might have been some singing and dancing involved."

His gaze narrowed. "That's not all, is it?"

Lani figured he had a right to know this, too, and was the only one who would understand why she did it. "I pretty much forced Russ to arrest me to keep him from carting you off to jail."

"He actually took you in?"

"Yup."

"Why would you do that? Lani, you should have let him come after me."

"I couldn't. Not with the legal challenge you're facing. If it wasn't about custody and visitation rights regarding your child, I would have stayed out of it. But you can't afford any black marks, or even gray ones, on your record."

His mouth thinned to an angry line. "I'm the one being judged even though Ginnie never saw fit to inform me that I was going to be a father."

"No one ever said life would be fair." That was all Lani could think to say. It wasn't fair that Russ was going to hate her when—if—he figured out she'd taken his keys. And it really wasn't fair that he'd kissed her and she'd responded and both of them lost control when they were locked up together.

"You okay, Lani?" Anderson gave her a funny look. "All of a sudden you went pale as a ghost."

"Fine. Part of the hangover that for no apparent reason is shaping up to be epidemic." She couldn't think about the *what-ifs* or *if onlys* right now. Her brother was going through a crisis. "Surely the court will take everything into consideration. It should matter that your child's mother didn't tell you she was pregnant."

"I was cheated out of that moment, which was bad enough. But she kept this child's existence from me for ten years."

Lani couldn't begin to understand how he felt. But it was the weight of carrying this burden alone that had finally compelled him to confide in her when she caught him at a vulnerable moment. She would help him through it as best she could. Whatever he needed she would do, no questions asked.

"It's not right, Anderson, what happened to you. But it's done. All you can do now is fight for your rights. To do that you can't afford anything but a spotless record."

"You've got a point." He sighed. "But I hate that you're in trouble on account of me."

"Not really. I think I'm in the clear. After Gage let us out of the cell—"

"Us? You weren't alone?"

"That's not important." It was too early and she was too tired to go into it. "Gage pretty much gave me a free pass because he was too busy dealing with other stuff."

"Like what?"

"Not sure. But I think a lot of people in town are feeling the same mysterious hangover that we are this morning." She shrugged. "The sheriff just told me to keep my nose clean. I don't think there will be any charges."

"If that changes, Dad can probably help."

"He could help you, too, if you'd let him," she pointed out.

"I have my reasons." Anderson shook his head. "I'm just glad you're in the clear. I don't want you taking a fall for me."

"That's not your call," she said. "You'd do it for me or anyone else you love. Just like me, you'd protect your family and have their back."

"You're right." His eyes glittered fiercely. "It's what Daltons do. And that's why I don't want anyone else to know about this legal stuff. You can't say a word to anyone in the family."

"But, Anderson—"

"No." He raised his voice then glanced toward the stairs, clearly concerned he'd wake someone. "Child custody cases aren't Dad's field of expertise. If Mom found out, she'd get attached to the idea. You know how much she wants more grandkids. And if I lose, not seeing her grandchild would break her heart. I can't do that to them, Lani, not unless it goes my way and I get visitation rights. You promised not to say anything."

"And I won't." She put her hand on his arm and met his gaze. "No one is going to find out from me."

"Okay." He nodded. "I really appreciate this. And I owe you one."

"I think you're on the hook for more than one," she teased. "Going to jail for you should count more than that. I'm thinking you should give me whatever I want for the rest of my life."

He grinned. "Don't push your luck, little sister."

"I'd never dream of it."

"Seriously, kid, I hope spending the night in the slammer wasn't too bad."

"It was really hideous. I don't care what they say about orange being the new black, it's just not my color. And don't even get me started on the food and those mattresses—"

He reached over and yanked her ponytail. "You definitely have a flair for the dramatic. And while it's very entertaining, we need to get to the ranch."

"Right."

Why did she have to go and bring up the mattress where she'd slept with Russ Campbell? Kissing him was a highlight. Being in his arms had a very high degree of awesomeness. She almost wished he would decide to press charges. That would mean he'd have to speak to her again.

The chances were slim to none that he would drop by

the Ace in the Hole while she was working, so her best hope of seeing Detective Dreamy again was to break the law.

And she *really* wanted to see him again…

Chapter Four

September 1

Russ Campbell pulled his truck to a stop in front of the Rust Creek Falls sheriff's office. It was impossible to step foot in this building without remembering the night he'd held Lani Dalton in his arms. He'd broken so many rules to have her and, God help him, it had been everything he'd dreamed about. Then he'd found out that she'd stolen his keys, deliberately locking them both in.

The next morning when the sheriff's office dispatcher had cleaned up the cell, she'd found them under the mattress. It was clear and irrefutable evidence that she'd made a fool of him. It wasn't the first time a woman had done that, but he vowed it would be the last.

Unfortunately, Lani was still keeping him up nights. He told himself it was because of trying to figure out what she'd really been up to the night of the Fourth. The truth ran more along the lines of he ached to touch her again.

He hated himself for it, but every time something brought him to Rust Creek Falls, he had a devil of a time resisting the urge to stop by the Ace in the Hole to see her. For him it came under the heading of borrowing trouble, and that was never smart.

He got out of the truck and went into the building. Since Gage was still trying to fill the deputy position and the dispatcher had gone home at five, no one was in the main room. He walked over to the office Gage used and saw the door was open. The sheriff was behind his desk, poring over paperwork.

"Knock, knock." Russ rapped his knuckles on the open door.

The other man looked up. "Russ. Thanks for coming by."

"No problem. You said it was important."

"That's right." Gage tossed his pen on top of the papers. "Have a seat."

He grabbed a metal chair from against the wall and pulled it over. "What's up?"

"Folks here in town are still unnerved about what happened on the Fourth of July. Everyone I talked to swears they weren't drinking hard liquor that night but ended up drunk as a skunk."

"Yeah. Not long after that night, Will Clifton paid me a visit while I was at the precinct in Kalispell. He knows I fill in here and wanted to talk to me, said he believed that someone had spiked his wife's punch. But lots of people were three sheets to the wind that night, and he asked if I believed something was put right in the punch bowl."

"What did you tell him?" Gage asked.

"That I hadn't come to any conclusion yet." Russ rubbed a hand across his neck. "But when I'm here, folks still bring it up. I also spoke with Claire Wyatt and her husband, Levi. Both said they were acting out of character after drinking the punch. What you just said is pretty much the same thing I keep hearing."

It's what Lani had told him that night, but he'd assumed she was lying. That hadn't made a bit of difference to him in how much he'd wanted her. How dumb did that make him? Definitely not using his head.

"Yeah, I read your reports. Very thorough."

"The only common denominator I can see is the wedding punch. It was most likely spiked."

Gage nodded. "That's what I think, too. But we can't prove it. By the time the dust settled, all the evidence was poured out and washed up. There was no point in taking samples from people affected because it was out of their system by then. So we've got zero to go on."

"And the more time that passes, the harder it is to get at the truth." Russ knew from working numerous cases that the sooner a crime scene was cordoned off and investigated, the better chance there was of finding evidence and solving the case.

"You're right about that. In two months I've made no progress on the investigation. But Labor Day is next week. Halloween is coming. There will be kids' parties and adult get-togethers, usually some kind of a community event. People are worried that it could happen again."

"I can see why folks are skittish," Russ agreed.

"The thing is, I'm still short a deputy since the last one left to take a job in Helena."

"Big city has bigger problems."

Gage's gaze narrowed on him. "Is that the voice of experience?"

"Yeah."

"Want to talk about it?"

"No." Russ wanted to forget about the fact that he'd worked with some really good cops, but not one of them had his back when he needed it most.

"Okay, then." Gage leaned back in his chair. "In case you were wondering, I didn't call you here just to vent about this mess."

"Didn't think so."

Russ had known this man since high school. His parents grew and sold hay to ranches in the areas surrounding Boulder Junction and Rust Creek Falls. Russ had helped deliver it. At the Christensen ranch, Gage always helped him unload the bales and they'd hit it off. Ever since, he'd considered the sheriff a good friend.

There was worry in the other man's eyes. It wasn't unusual because he tended to be serious by nature, but the depth of the unease was reserved for really serious situations. Like the flood that had nearly destroyed Rust Creek Falls a couple years ago. And now this.

"I keep the peace here," Gage said. "I settle disputes, break up fights and make sure folks are safe. Right now they don't feel safe and are coming to me for answers. I don't have any, but I damned sure intend to get some."

"How?"

"I need your help on this, Russ. You're a detective and you were working on the night in question. You know how to conduct an investigation and piece information together to get the full picture." Gage's mouth pulled into a grim line for a moment. "I'm asking you to do that now. Part-time isn't enough but there's no choice, what with your job in Kalispell, but I'd really appreciate all you can give."

Russ didn't have to think it over very long. He quit his job in Denver after blowing the whistle on a dirty cop there, and then it became too dangerous to stay. So he'd come back to Montana and applied for a position with Kalispell PD. Gage had given him a glowing recommendation and since he was in the law enforcement field, his opinion carried a lot of weight.

Russ had a career thanks to this man, who gave him

a hand up at a low point in his life. He would always be grateful for that.

"I'm in," he said simply. "I haven't taken a vacation for at least two years, not since starting in Kalispell. Between that and personal days, I can give you a month of full-time work." He thought for a moment. "If I stay here in town, folks might open up to me more easily than if I come and go."

Gage nodded thoughtfully. "Strickland's Boarding House might have a room, and if not, Lissa and I would be happy to put you up."

"I'll try Strickland's." Russ was reluctant to impose on the couple who hadn't been married all that long.

"Good. Thanks, Russ. I owe you."

"No. This might put us somewhere in the neighborhood of even for what you did to help me." He cleared his throat. "So the working theory is that someone spiked the punch. That would suggest this person wanted to make a public statement to a good portion of the population. It's personal, but not focused on a single individual."

"Yeah." Gage nodded.

"We have to consider whether or not someone has a grudge against the whole town."

"Makes sense," the sheriff agreed.

"A lot of different people drank that punch." Russ was thinking out loud. He kept the reference general even though a picture of Lani Dalton popped into his mind, sassy and sexy and tipsy in her soaked sundress. "Business types. Ranchers. Young parents." He was thinking about Claire and Levi Wyatt. "Finding a common thread between them all could be a challenge."

"Especially for someone who isn't familiar with the quirks and personalities of folks in this town."

Russ knew that was directed at him and remembered Lani saying he was an outsider, although looking back, some of the nature of that talk could have been due to the effects of the spiked punch.

"Maybe it's not a good idea for me to be the investigator on this. What if I handle the routine calls and you do the footwork, ask the questions? We can collaborate on what you find out."

Gage thought for a moment then shook his head. "Some day-to-day situations here can get delicate, and knowing history and temperament can keep a small dustup from turning into a full-blown feud. I need a guy like you asking the questions. You're trained to read between the lines, to look for connections that aren't obvious. Not knowing people could be a plus. You might see things I'd miss."

"Okay. I'll do my best, poke around and find out what people saw. Surely not everyone was drunk off their butt that night. Who knows what they might have witnessed? And I have the impression that in this town, no one keeps anything to themselves for long."

He remembered Lani saying as much to him when they were stuck in the cell. Well, not stuck so much as her making a fool out of him. She could have given him back the key at any time.

What was her game? Why did she sleep with him? Because she wanted to—or was there an ulterior motive?

"I just had an idea." Gage snapped his fingers. "People do talk, and they do a good portion of that talking at the Ace in the Hole."

"Okay." Russ nodded. "I'll chat up Rosey Traven. She's the owner of the place."

The sheriff didn't look convinced. "Because she *is* the owner, she's not necessarily interacting with the clientele. Someone who primarily works with the customers is a better option."

"Good point. I've been in there from time to time, so

I know a couple of the waitresses. Annie Kellerman and Liza Bradley."

Russ had struck up conversations with both women. Each was pretty enough but they weren't Lani. He deliberately stayed clear of her and that was smart, as it turned out. One conversation with her and they couldn't keep their hands off each other.

Gage shook his head. "Neither of them has been in town that long. I think you should start with Lani Dalton. She knows everyone and might have overheard something."

Color Russ surprised. "Do I have to remind you that her behavior on the night in question was suspicious? You're aware that she deliberately took my keys and hid them to take me out of commission."

Gage laughed. "There were an awful lot of good, upstanding people who did weird things that night because of the spiked punch. She was a victim, too, don't forget. Whatever her reasons, I'd bet my badge her intentions were not about breaking the law. She's salt of the earth." A gleam stole into the other man's eyes. "Maybe she just had the hots for you, Russ, and wanted to get you alone to have her way with you."

That was right on the mark, and Russ had to wonder which of them was the better detective. And, for the record, Lani didn't have her way with him. He'd actually started it and was a willing and eager participant.

Russ couldn't quite meet the other man's gaze when he said, "She's a piece of work."

"Like the rest of her family," Gage said. "But I can tell you that she's never been in trouble."

"I'll have to take your word for that, Sheriff."

"Then take it on this, too. Talk to Lani. Start the investigation with her."

Russ stood up. "Is that an order?"

"It can be. But let's call it gut instinct."

"Okay, then. It's your town. We'll do it your way."

And wasn't this a fine mess. The moment he'd laid eyes on Lani he knew getting close to her would be borrowing trouble. The time had come to look trouble in her big, brown eyes and hope it didn't expect to be paid back.

So, after months of avoiding her, his job was to talk to the woman he had no reason to trust. The hell of it was that the person he mistrusted the most was himself.

It was just about quitting time for most people in and around Rust Creek Falls, and sometimes they stopped by the Ace in the Hole. But it was Tuesday and Lani never knew how busy her shift would be. She was getting ready for whoever showed up, filling napkin holders and saltshakers at the booths and tables.

Glancing out the window she saw the hitching post, where cowboys could tie up their horses when they rode in. Lighted beer signs in the window signaled the type of establishment this was as did the oversize ace-of-hearts playing card that blinked in red neon.

The screen door had rusty hinges and screeched every time it was opened and worked just fine as a signal for alerting them that a customer had arrived. Behind her the bar ran the length of the wall and had stools in front of it. Anyone sitting there looked into a mirror mounted on the wall, where the bottles of liquor lined up in front of it were reflected. Booths ringed the outer wall and circular tables big enough for six surrounded the dance floor in the middle of the room. In a couple of hours the place could be jammed with people ready to shake off the stress of the workday. Or not.

There were a few people in the place already. A couple lingering over a late lunch, holding hands and giving each other adoring—and annoying—smiles. There were a few guys nursing beers at the bar, but Lani focused in on Wes

Eggleston, recently split from his wife. He was looking at his beer as if wishing he could dive in headfirst. Rosey, her boss, was in the back with her husband, supposedly taking inventory, but Lani guessed they were taking inventory of each other. More than once she'd caught them making out like a couple of teenagers. She envied the bond they had—both business and personal.

Lani was handling bartending and waitressing duties until Annie Kellerman arrived to take care of drink orders. The bartender had called in and said she was going to be a little late tonight. Glancing at Wes again, Lani felt kind of sorry for him and walked behind the bar, stopping in front of where he was slumped.

"Hey, Wes, can I get you some water?"

His eyes were sad and bloodshot. "No, thanks."

"How are things with you and Kathy?"

"Separation's not doing it for her. She wants a divorce. Told me today."

That explained a lot. "I'm sorry," she said. The couple had a three-year-old daughter. "Any chance you two can work things out?"

He shrugged. "She wanted me to go to counseling. But I said no."

"Why is that?" Lani saw stubborn slide into his expression and held up her hand. "Sorry. It's none of my business. You don't have to talk about it if you don't want to."

"Nah. It's okay." He shrugged again. "I just don't see how telling a stranger our problems is going to solve 'em."

The screen door behind her screeched and slammed shut, but whoever it was could wait just a minute.

"I don't know, either," she said to Wes. "But what can it hurt to talk to someone? An objective stranger could give you some things to think about."

"Seems like nonsense to me," he said stubbornly.

She scooped ice into a glass then squirted soda water

into it. After dropping a lime into the bubbly liquid, she set it on the bar beside his beer bottle.

"If you don't do anything, it's over, right? So you've got nothing to lose by trying it Kathy's way. And if it turns out to be nonsense like you say, no harm, no foul. At least someday you can tell your little girl you tried everything to keep her family together."

He stared at her for several moments then nodded. "Never thought about it like that."

"See?" She smiled. "Talking to someone can change your perspective, get you to see things differently. Can't fix a problem you don't know about."

"I'll consider it. Thanks, Lani."

"Don't mention it." She set a paper-wrapped straw beside his soda water. "Let me know if you need anything else."

She half turned to the new arrival and said, "Sorry to keep you waiting, I—"

The words stuck in her throat when she saw Russ Campbell in all his worn-jeans, snug-T-shirt and leather-jacket-wearing glory. Last time she'd seen him, the town was all dressed up in red, white and blue, in the full swing of summer. Now Labor Day was a week away and fall just around the corner. She might not have seen him since *that* night, but she'd thought about him plenty.

At first when she worked a shift, every time that squeaky screen door opened, her stomach dropped as if she was riding the jackhammer at the county fair. But he never showed. After a few weeks of that adrenaline roller coaster, disappointment settled in and she was torn between wondering what might have been and relief that it turned out to be nothing.

Now *nothing* was sitting at the bar in front of her.

"Hi, Lani." That voice was smooth as dark chocolate

mixed with expensive Scotch. Those hazel eyes studied her intently.

She couldn't believe he was really here, had convinced herself that he would never darken her doorway again. Let alone voluntarily speak to her. He wasn't ignoring her. "It's been a while."

"I'm here on official business."

So, his talking to her wasn't voluntary; he was here as a cop. "Just when I thought I'd beaten the rap, you talked Gage into filing charges against me for my fountain dance. Isn't there a statute of limitations on that?"

"This isn't about the fountain." One corner of his mouth curved up. "But I am here about what happened on the Fourth of July."

Her heart pounded. Maybe he'd been thinking about her, too. Heat filled her when she glanced at his wide chest, and memories of him holding her came rushing back. "Oh?"

"A lot of folks have reported drinking the wedding reception punch and getting drunk then doing things that were out of character."

"Like me?" She couldn't manage to keep a little bit of I told you-so out of her voice.

"Yeah," he said. "Like you. We're pretty sure someone put something right in the punch."

"That's a sobering thought, no pun intended. Who would do that?" Chills prickled through her. "Why?"

"Don't know. But Gage hired me as an investigator to find out."

"Don't you have another job?" She knew he did. He was a detective. She almost winced, remembering when she'd called him Detective Dreamy. Out loud. It was the truth, but still…

"I'm taking a month's leave to handle this."

"Now you're scaring me. The sheriff's really that concerned?"

Russ nodded. "The who and why are important. If someone has a grudge against Rust Creek Falls, there could be another incident. Labor Day is coming up. There will be picnics and public celebrations. If someone wants to cause harm, it's another opportunity."

"Oh, my gosh—"

"Then there are more holidays—Halloween. Thanksgiving. Christmas. All of them traditionally have community events attached. I'm going to get to the bottom of this before then." His expression was determined. "And I'm starting with you."

"Me?" She blinked at him. "You don't seriously believe I was responsible for that?"

"I don't know for sure who did it, but it's not like you didn't stir up trouble that night."

It was the first time ever, but that was splitting hairs. "You say trouble, I say...mischief. I had some of that spiked punch and was experiencing a sensation of...happy."

And feeling no fear.

"You call stealing the keys to the jail cell and locking me in while I was on duty *mischief*?"

"Me?" Maybe she could bluff. "Someone else could have—"

"Don't." He held up a hand. "They were under the mattress."

It didn't seem as if he was in the mood to be teased out of being mad about this. She'd wondered if that's what had kept him from coming back to the Ace in the Hole. The suspicion on his face told her she might be onto something.

"I'm sorry, Russ."

"Really?" He didn't sound convinced. "Anyone else would have used them to get out of jail, not hidden them to stay locked *in*. The question is why you would do that? What were you up to?"

That night she'd had her brother's back, but she couldn't

tell him. "I would never do anything to hurt anyone, especially the people here in Rust Creek Falls. They're my friends and neighbors."

He looked at her for several moments, assessing her sincerity, no doubt. She really hoped those eyes of his didn't miss anything, because she was being absolutely straight about this.

"Gage vouched for you." He rested his forearms on the edge of the scarred bar. "But I've learned not to take anything or anyone at face value."

Needing something to do with her hands, she grabbed a damp rag and used it to wipe the already clean wooden surface in front of him. "That sounds really cynical."

"I've got my reasons."

A girl didn't deal with the public as much as Lani without picking up instincts about people. Some of what happened that night was fuzzy, but other things were crystal clear. She remembered how he'd guessed about her bad relationship experience, and she was going to return the favor. "Spoken like a man who's been dumped. Want to talk about it?"

The tough cop facade slipped for a second, then he recovered. And ignored the offer. "My job is all about dealing with people who break the law then lie through their teeth. If that doesn't entitle a guy to be wary, I don't know what does."

"I suppose."

"Look, Gage sent me here to talk to you. He says you know pretty much everyone in town, and you're an astute judge of character. That you might be able to shed some light on what went on that day. Maybe someone had a little too much to drink and started bragging. Maybe you've overheard something that would give us a lead."

Lani thought for a moment, but knew something like

that would have stuck in her mind. She shook her head. "If I had, I'd have brought it to Gage's attention right away."

"Okay, then." He slid off the stool, apparently anxious to get away from her.

"But Gage is right. I do know everyone. And I can read people pretty well, unless romantic feelings are involved," she said ruefully. She'd completely misread the guy who walked out on her.

"So I was right about you getting dumped." His gaze held hers. "Want to talk about it?"

"Wow, a man willing to listen. That's a surprise." She folded her arms over her chest. "But, as you said, it's part of your job description."

"Pretty much."

"Well, you're off the hook, Detective. I don't want to talk about it except to say that my romantic life consists of listening to the sad stories of folks who come into the bar here."

"Yeah. I heard you talking to that guy on the end."

She glanced over her shoulder and saw Wes finishing off his water. "It's even sadder when kids are caught in the middle."

"I know what you mean." He rested his palm flat on the bar. "Okay, then. If you do hear anything, can I count on you to pass it along to someone in law enforcement?"

"Of course. But I really want to help find whoever did this."

"Get in line."

"Seriously. Like I said, I know nearly everyone in town. I have information about things that happened way back when. Feuds, fights, disagreements. Someone who might have a reason to do harm. I could be of help."

"That's okay—"

"Look, Russ, I understand why you don't trust me, but Gage assured you that I'm on the up and up. Don't blow off a potential resource because of what happened." Heat burned up her neck and into her cheeks because the list of sins under the heading of *what happened* included sleeping with him. She couldn't go there.

"This is my town," she continued, "and I have a personal stake in helping to protect the people here that I care deeply about. You know you'd never forgive yourself if someone got hurt and you didn't do everything possible. I know I wouldn't."

"I understand what you're saying, Lani, but—"

She held up her hand to stop him from saying no. "In the spirit of fair disclosure, you should know that I'm going to do it anyway. I'll keep my ears open and ask questions. So you can either let me work with you or I'll just go rogue."

"Go rogue?" Suddenly, he smiled and looked completely adorable.

"Yes." All her girlie places tingled, and she wanted to flirt like crazy. Too bad she'd burned that bridge in a jail cell. "It's up to you."

He looked at her for a long, assessing moment. Finally, reluctantly, he said, "Okay."

"Great. We need to talk about—"

"Not here." He looked around. "Anyone could overhear."

"Right. This is too public. So we need to find a place where no one can eavesdrop." She thought for a moment. "Can you ride a horse?"

"Yes. I'm a farm boy, remember?"

She nodded. "Okay. Meet me at the ranch tomorrow. Around noon. I guarantee I can find a place where no one can listen in."

"Okay. If you need me, I'm staying at Strickland's Boarding House for the next month. I'll see you tomorrow."

Lani couldn't wait.

Chapter Five

Damn his protective instincts, Russ thought, as the horse he was riding kept pace with Lani's. If not for that, he would be at the sheriff's office in Rust Creek Falls mapping out an investigation strategy on his own. But he'd seen her bullheaded single-mindedness for himself and couldn't let her go rogue on this. Until they knew who was responsible for spiking the wedding punch, the motive was a mystery. He couldn't risk Lani working on her own and getting hurt.

So, at the appointed time, he'd met her at the Dalton ranch, where she'd had two horses saddled and waiting for their ride.

"It's awfully quiet over there."

Russ looked at her and waited for the thump in his chest that always happened when he looked at her. He felt it and sincerely wished he hadn't.

"I'm using all my powers of concentration to stay in the saddle."

"Oh, please," she scoffed. "You sit a horse as well as my brothers do, and that's their job."

"You're not so bad yourself."

She looked sexy all the time but, for some reason, even more so on the black-and-white pinto pony named Valentino. Worn jeans covered her legs, but there was something even more tempting about what he couldn't see. Her hair was in a French braid that hung down her back, and a brown Stetson protected her head and face from the sun.

She met his gaze. "Riding a horse is my job, too."

So she'd told him while they shared a jail cell where they'd done a whole lot more than talk. The problem was he really wanted to do a whole lot more again. He'd come back to Montana to kick-start his stalled career. Spending time with Lani had distracted him just as he'd suspected it would the first time he laid eyes on her. Now he was forced to interact with her—which gave him greater incentive to solve this case quickly.

Russ realized they were heading for the local waterfall when he heard the sound of rushing water. They crossed a wooden bridge and rounded a bend in the mountain trail. After lazily moving through a stand of trees, he saw the clearing and the waterfall for which Rust Creek Falls had been named. At the base there was a pool ringed by rocks. It would be a romantic spot with the right person. That was a dangerous thought in itself, since he'd been unable to resist this woman in a jail cell, which was the polar opposite of romantic.

"No one will overhear us here," Lani said.

In a grassy area she stopped her horse and slid off then led Valentino over to the pool for a drink of water. Russ followed her lead.

He patted the neck of his mahogany horse. "Coming all the way out here might be an overabundance of caution."

"Maybe. But it's a spectacular day, and I never get tired

of looking at the falls. I call that a win-win." She looked around and breathed deeply of the clean air.

His gaze settled on the chest of her plaid, snap-front shirt and the way it perfectly fit her full breasts and trim waist. Another spectacular view and a definite win-win.

But that wasn't why they'd come here.

After the horses finished drinking, they ground-tied the animals near the grass so they could graze.

"Okay," he said, "about the investigation—"

"Hold on." She grabbed a cloth bag and a blanket roll tied to the back of her saddle. "I packed lunch. Don't know about you, but I'm starving, and I can't think on an empty stomach."

Russ was hungry, too, and not just for food. Deliberately avoiding her since that night in jail hadn't done anything to diminish his wanting her, and seeing her last night had only made things worse. But it had been thoughtful of her to pack lunch for them.

"Thanks, that would be great." He took the blanket from her and spread it out under a shady tree.

Lani sat cross-legged then handed him an apple, a small bag of chips and a sandwich, then she took hers out of the plastic bag. "Hope you like ham. And if you're a mayonnaise hater, you're not going to be a happy camper."

"I'm good with it." He pulled one of the sandwich triangles out of the bag. The fact that she'd cut it in half struck him as a womanly touch, not something he, or any guy he knew for that matter, would do. It was nice.

"Okay, then." She took a bite of hers and they ate in silence, the only sounds in the clearing coming from the waterfall rushing over the rocks on the side of the mountain. Or the occasional chirp of a bird.

"I've come up with a list of suspects," she said, after chewing the last of her sandwich.

"What criteria did you use?"

"Incidents from that night." She held up three fingers and ticked them off. "A couple got married. Another split up. And a ranch was won in a poker game. That's just for starters."

"I'm aware of the first two," he said. "A week or so after they got married during the reception, Will Clifton approached me about the possibility that his wife, Jordyn Leigh, was drugged at the wedding."

"Did *he* act guilty?"

"No." In Russ's opinion, he'd behaved like a man who was looking out for the woman he loved. "And I talked to Claire Wyatt about the fight she had with her husband."

"And?" Lani took a bite of the apple.

Russ couldn't seem to take his eyes off her mouth and the small bit of apple juice on her lower lip. The urge to lick that drop was almost irresistible.

"Russ?"

"Hmm?"

"You started to tell me what Claire had to say," she prompted.

"Right." If he didn't keep his head in the game, this investigation was going to take three times as long. "She didn't tell me anything that would shed light on who might have doctored the punch."

He'd taken notes during each interview and added them to his own observations from that night. Will and Claire both said that their partners'—and their own—behavior had been out of character and consistent with being drunk even though they hadn't consumed any hard alcohol. Russ had noticed an awful lot of people were feeling no pain that night even before he'd arrested Lani.

"I think the Cliftons and the Wyatts were victims. Like you," he added before she could say anything. She was innocent as far as how she'd become intoxicated, but stealing the cell keys to detain him was not so easily explained.

"It doesn't make sense that Claire or Levi Wyatt would have anything to gain by getting the whole town drunk. He's just feeling the pressure of providing for his family. A wife and baby is a lot of responsibility."

"Being young parents doesn't automatically make them innocent," he pointed out.

"True. But I just don't see either of them doing something like that. What possible motive could they have?"

He agreed, but couldn't resist needling her. "I don't think your gut instinct would exonerate them in a court of law. Hard evidence is the only thing that matters."

"If you had any evidence, hard or otherwise, we wouldn't be here now."

"True enough." And as much as he wanted to mind being here with her, he couldn't seem to manage it.

"We have to look at who had something to gain by getting everyone drunk." Lani leaned back against the tree trunk and stretched her legs out in front of her.

"So, let's talk about that poker game."

She put her apple core in the empty plastic bag and started on the chips. "Old Boyd Sullivan gambled away his property to Brad Crawford in a really high-stakes game that was apparently going on at the Ace in the Hole."

"That's definitely motive." He met her gaze. "Anything else?"

"Jordyn Leigh Cates married Will Clifton that night. Rust Creek Ramblings got a lot of mileage out of that story."

"What is Rust Creek Ramblings?" This is where a local could really help.

"It's a gossip column in the *Rust Creek Falls Gazette*, written by someone who apparently wishes to remain anonymous, because there's no name on the articles." There was a gleam in her eyes that had nothing to do with the sun peeking through overhead tree branches. "Whoever it is has gotten a lot of juicy stuff from what happened at that wedding reception."

"That's also motive," he pointed out, carefully watching her.

"I guess so."

"You know everyone in town and their business. Could it be that you're the one who writes Rust Creek Ramblings?"

"You're not serious," she scoffed.

"Dead serious."

She looked at him for several moments then laughed. "Let me point out the holes in that theory. A lot of stuff in those columns was about things that happened while I was in jail with you." The shadow of her hat couldn't hide the pink that stained her cheeks.

"Let me point out the hole in that alibi. You could have gotten information to write about from anyone you talked to at the bar."

"True. But I didn't." She shrugged. "When would I have time to write it down? I'm up before God to work on the ranch and I have the other job."

"Part-time." He leaned back on his hands and stretched his legs out. His boots nearly touched hers, making this more intimate than he wanted. "When you have the gossip, how long could it take to knock out the column?"

"Hmm." She nodded thoughtfully. "I can see how you'd come to that conclusion, but I don't write it."

"If that's not a lie," he said, giving her a pointed look, "then I would really like to know who does. They seem to have a whole lot of facts about what happened that night. It could save a lot of time on this investigation."

"So you're anxious to have it over and be rid of me?"

"I didn't say that." Didn't mean she wasn't right, though. "But solving this would put people's minds at ease."

"Right." She nodded. "Okay. Be skeptical. It's probably mandatory for a detective. And, for the record, I don't blame you for suspecting me, but I didn't do it. So don't waste too much time looking in the wrong direction. Now, back to the case… It's common knowledge that hairstylists and bartenders know everyone's business."

A good deal of Russ's detective work was done by observing people. In his experienced opinion, Lani wasn't at all concerned about being a suspect. Either she was innocent or she was a very accomplished liar.

"Moving on," she said. "Let's go back to Jordyn and Will. They got married."

"And here's where your knowledge of the key players comes in handy. Do you think she would drug an entire town to get a man to marry her?"

"It wasn't a secret that she moved to Rust Creek Falls hoping to meet someone and get married. But she already knew Will from Thunder Canyon." She was thinking out loud then shook her head. "Since she works with children at Country Kids Day Care, I'd like to think she would never do something like that."

"But you can't be sure?"

"No."

"It's not a good idea to let it slide, then. I'll talk to her."

"That would be best," she agreed.

"And I think you should be there when I do." He was trying really hard to believe he'd said that for the good of the investigation and not personal reasons. "Since people seem to feel comfortable spilling their guts to you."

He'd seen it for himself when he went to the Ace in the Hole last night. That cowboy at the bar was talking to her about marriage counseling, and he admired the way she'd gotten through to him.

"Okay. I can do that," she agreed.

"And what about Brad Crawford? Do you think he's capable of something that underhanded?"

"Good question." She tapped her lip thoughtfully.

"Where real estate is involved, the Crawfords can get intense, but..."

"Okay. He can't be ruled out, either."

"No," she agreed.

She had to go and tap her lips, distracting him again. He'd had about as much of this brainstorming session as his willpower could take.

"I need to get back to the sheriff's office," he said abruptly.

"Okay. Yeah—" She stood up and started gathering their trash. "Me, too. Back to work, I mean. I have stuff to do this afternoon."

After Russ rolled to his feet, he had the damnedest urge to pull her into his arms and kiss the living daylights out of her. If only his protective streak extended to protecting her from him or saving him from himself.

He'd included her in his investigation to keep her out of trouble, but spending time with her was its own kind of danger. Wasn't that the classic definition of a catch-22?

"Did you have any trouble getting the evening off?" Russ kept his eyes on the road.

"Since I wasn't scheduled at the bar tonight, it wasn't a problem." Lani glanced over at him, sitting in the driver's seat of his truck.

He'd picked her up at home, and they were on the way to Jordyn Leigh and Will Clifton's ranch, which was located east of Rust Creek Falls. She was fascinated by his hands on the steering wheel—so competent, in control, strong.

The memory of those hands touching her bare skin was vivid and had desire curling through her. The sensations he'd coaxed from her that night seemed a lifetime ago, and she craved them for a second time. But since he'd turned up in her life again, he'd given no indication that he even remembered the passion that had so easily flared between them. Maybe it was best that she try to forget, too.

"Does Jordyn Leigh know we're coming?" she asked.

He nodded. "I called her and explained that there are still questions about what happened that night. She mentioned that Will was busy with work and wouldn't be there, so I told her you would be with me. I thought that would put her more at ease."

"Did you tell her that I'm helping with the investigation?"

"No. For two reasons. First, if word gets out that you're narcing, the flow of potentially helpful information will dry up. And second—again if word gets out—you could be in danger from whoever is responsible for what happened."

"So what did you tell her?" She looked at him. "About why I'm here, I mean."

"Nothing."

"Really?"

He glanced at her, and his expression was seriously annoyed. "She didn't ask."

Lani shook her head. "Here's the thing—Jordyn Leigh is a woman, and unless she's a quart low on estrogen, she's going to wonder what the heck I'm doing on this ride-along. There's a reason people are talking about that gossip columnist and buying the *Gazette* to read the columns. This is a small town, Russ, and they're curious about what's going on with everyone else."

"Okay, you have a point." A muscle jerked in his jaw. "Then I guess we should have a cover story in case she asks."

"She's going to ask," Lani assured him.

"Any suggestions?"

"It has to be personal, otherwise I'm on official business, and then the word would be out that I'm a narc, as you put it."

The corners of his mouth curved up and for just a moment there was the possibility of a smile that would blossom into adorableness. Then he turned serious again.

"Can't fault your logic. So, on the off chance she asks—" he gave her a quick, pointed look "—I stopped by the Ace in the Hole, saw you and asked you to dinner. We're going right after I interview her."

Lani was more than a little annoyed at his selective memory. Considering he'd been showing up where she worked for months and barely talked to her, then suddenly lightning strikes? That story was pathetic. At least from her point of view.

"She'll have more questions."

"Like what?"

"I'm not psychic." Maybe Lani was projecting because *she* had a lot of questions. Like during all these months, had he been more aware of her than he'd let on? Had he thought about asking her out and just never did? If so, why not? But she couldn't ask any of that. "It's just that she's had a lot of time since your phone call to think about what you told her and wonder about the two of us."

"We'll have to cross that bridge when we come to it because we're almost there."

They'd been driving on a road with acres of rolling green land dotted here and there by stands of cottonwood, pine and oak. The sun was low in the sky, just above Fall Mountain and the snowcapped peaks of the Rockies. The ranch compound came into view and included the main house, foreman's cottage, a bunkhouse, barn and corrals. There were a series of fenced pastures close by.

He drove through the open gate, underneath an arch that said "Flying C." Beyond that Lani spotted the two-story, white-sided, blue-shuttered farmhouse with a wraparound porch. There were lights glowing in the windows. It was after six o'clock, and the sun finally disappeared behind the mountains, bathing everything in shadow.

Russ parked the truck in front of the place. "Remember, don't say too much. Let her do the talking."

"Trust me. I've had a lot of experience with that." Of all people, he should know that sometimes a person just didn't say much of anything. That was his standard operating procedure with Lani at the Ace in the Hole.

Side by side they walked up the newly repaired steps to the door, which had a shiny new coat of paint and a fan-shaped window set into the wall above it. Russ knocked lightly, and Jordyn Leigh answered moments later. She was a pretty blonde who looked as if she didn't have a deceptive bone in her body.

"Hi, Detective Campbell. Come in."

The door opened to a small foyer with stairs in the center that led to the upper floor. There was a living room to the left and dining room on the right. The floor was wide-planked hardwood that looked freshly refinished, and the old-fashioned sash windows would let in lots of sunlight.

Jordyn Leigh stood back and let them by. "Can I get you something to drink? Coffee? Iced tea?"

"Appreciate it, but no," Russ told her. "This won't take long. We don't want to keep you."

"It's very sweet of you to help," Lani added.

Jordyn Leigh smiled warmly. "Lani, I haven't seen you in a while."

Lani looked around. Word on the street in Rust Creek Falls was that this place had been a mess when they moved in, but the two of them had worked hard to fix it up fast. The inside looked brand-new now and incredibly homey. She envied the newlyweds, finding each other and building a future together.

"I guess you've been pretty busy settling into married life," Lani said.

"That's for sure. I've been taking online classes for my degree in early childhood development on top of cleaning, repairing and upgrading this house." Jordyn Leigh's blue eyes sparkled with happiness. "I was surprised when the detective said you'd be here, Lani. How long have you two known each other?"

Lani knew that was a polite way of asking how long they'd been dating. But since she'd been instructed not to say much, she looked at Russ, indicating he should field the question.

"Well," he said, "it's a small town. You know how that is."

He could have said they weren't dating but that would make her presence here more curious. Probably he was hoping to avoid any finer points to explain her tagging along, but no way that was going to fly, Lani thought. She decided to embellish.

"We officially met at the big wedding reception, when he arrested me for dancing in the fountain."

"I heard about that." Curiosity was obvious in the other woman's eyes.

"Technically I took her in for resisting arrest." The look on Russ's face indicated he still wondered why she'd done that.

Jordyn Leigh smiled. "Sounds like there's an interesting story there."

"You don't know the half of it," Lani said. "We've gotten to know each other pretty well since then."

She felt Russ's disapproval and realized that his body language did not scream of his attraction to her. Either he was lousy at undercover assignments or he just didn't like her. Too bad. There was more at stake here than his delicate sensibilities. They needed to look as if they at least liked each other. And she couldn't resist messing with him a little.

She moved closer and leaned her head against his

shoulder. "You'd be surprised how romantic a jail cell can be. Right, Russ?"

His eyes narrowed, but he turned into Detective Adorable and smiled that special smile as he slid an arm around her waist. "Don't spread that around."

"I wouldn't dream of it."

"So, this is an official visit?" Jordyn Leigh asked. "You wanted to ask me about the night of the Traub-MacCallum wedding?"

"That's right," Russ said.

"You didn't really have to drag Lani along for this. I feel completely comfortable with anyone Sheriff Christensen trusts."

Lani knew there was a question buried in that statement and sent him an I-told-you-so look. She was going to cross that bridge he'd mentioned, and this would probably not make him happy.

"We're heading out to dinner after this. And it's so sweet. He wanted me to ride along with him. Keep him company."

"That's right." His voice had a slight edge to it.

"Very sweet." The other woman smiled. "What did you want to ask?"

Russ removed his arm from Lani's waist. "Sounds like you and your husband just moved in."

"We did. Right after we got married on the Fourth."

"By all accounts, that was sudden. Did you know Will was buying property when you married him?"

"Yes. We talked about it when I bumped into him at the wedding reception." She frowned. "Why do you ask?"

"It's a nice spread, and he's got plans to really make something of it." Russ stopped and looked at the new bride.

Lani recognized that this was his interrogation style and knew he was getting at a motive for spiking the punch. She knew this tough detective tactic was the fastest way to alienate Jordyn Leigh and shut off the free flow of information.

Lani made a stab at damage control. "You moved here from Thunder Canyon a couple years ago, right? Didn't you and Will know each other there?"

"We grew up together. I had a crush on him for a while, but he always treated me like a kid sister." Her eyes sparkled at the memory.

"So, when he showed up here in town for the wedding, did you think about giving him a push in a direction you wanted him to go?" Russ asked.

Lani wanted to elbow him in the ribs. He was about as subtle as a sledgehammer. Probably this approach worked with a hardened criminal in the precinct interrogation room while half the force was watching from the other side of the two-way window. But on someone as sweet and innocent as Jordyn Leigh Cates—now Clifton—it was going to backfire. She needed a lighter touch.

"What Russ means is, something must have shifted for Will, because it's all over town how much in love the two of you are," Lani said. "Talk about romantic. Since you two knew each other before, it can't be love at first sight. More like being struck by lightning?"

"Good question," Jordyn Leigh admitted. "I remember Will taking my punch away and implying that I was tipsy. But that was impossible because it's a public park and there's no hard liquor allowed."

"That didn't stop some folks," Russ interjected.

"Will said the same thing. But I was miffed and just got up and got another cup for myself. I poured him some, too, and we hung out the rest of the night."

"And what happened?" Lani asked.

"It's fuzzy after that. My next clear memory is waking up in the morning. With a monster hangover and a marriage license."

Russ nodded and his cop face relaxed. "The sheriff and I think the punch was spiked."

"Will thought mine was. I remember that from the reception. Before I don't remember anything," Jordyn Leigh said ruefully.

"Do you have any idea who might have wanted to get half the town wasted?" Lani asked.

The other woman shook her head. "But I have to say…"

"What?" Russ asked.

"I know you've been hired to find out what happened, and that folks are nervous, thinking someone is up to no good. I truly hope no one was seriously hurt that night, but Will and I would like to thank whoever did it. We found each other, thanks to that punch. It got us together, and he's the love of my life. We feel very blessed."

"Okay." Russ nodded politely. "I appreciate your time."

"If I can be of any further help, let me know," she said.

"Tell Will I said hello," Lani told her as they walked out the door.

"Absolutely. You two have a nice dinner." Jordyn Leigh smiled and waved.

Russ handed her into the truck then walked around to the driver's side and got in. "Just as I suspected. There's no way she's responsible."

"I agree." But something Jordyn Leigh said stuck with Lani. "Was anyone badly injured that night?"

"Not that we know of. Why?"

"Because it could just be a onetime prank. Or a case could be made that because there were no major consequences, another incident might be in the works."

"Gage and I had the same thought," Russ acknowledged.

"You could have said something."

"That theory could panic folks and is better not made public," he said.

"I see your point. What a mess."

At least Jordyn Leigh and Will found love and got a happy ending out of that night. They got together. Lani and Russ did, too, but love had nothing to do with it, and now he acted as if nothing had happened. She didn't know what to make of that.

If she were a man maybe she could pretend nothing of consequence took place. But she wasn't a man and was irritated that he didn't seem the least bit interested in her.

Still, there was no doubt in her mind that word would spread about their going out to dinner. She got more than a little satisfaction from the fact that to maintain this cover while working on his case, he would have to deal with her. Up close and personal.

Chapter Six

Russ opened the squeaky screen door at the Ace in the Hole and walked inside. He scanned the dimly lit interior for Lani as he always did, as he couldn't seem to avoid doing. If there was a way to keep himself from looking for her, he hadn't found it yet. But tonight he needed to talk to her. It had been a couple of days since the interview with Jordyn Leigh Clifton, and so far he hadn't come up with anything new. He was really hoping Lani had picked up something here at her job that would give him a lead to go on.

It was Saturday night of Labor Day weekend, and the place was more crowded than normal. The upcoming holiday gave him a sense of urgency in solving this mystery. He and Gage would be vigilant for the public community picnic in the park, but they couldn't be everywhere.

He finally spotted Lani delivering baskets of fries and burgers to a table where four cowboys were seated. She chatted with them for a few moments, laughing and smiling at whatever was said. If he didn't miss his guess, there was some major-league flirting on both sides.

She was single; Russ had no claim on her. But that didn't stop something dark and dangerous from coiling in his gut.

He walked through the place on his way to the bar and could tell exactly when most of the people inside knew the lawman had arrived. Conversation nearly stopped, and the noise level dropped noticeably. Everyone looked at him suspiciously. He was conscious of the change because that's the way the guys at his precinct in Denver had looked at him after he'd ratted out a dirty cop.

The circumstances were different, but obviously word had spread in Rust Creek Falls that he was working for Sheriff Christensen and asking questions in an official capacity.

He nodded to Lani on the way by and gave each of those overexcited cowboys a look with a message every guy understood: back off. Then he walked over to the bar and took the stool on the end that was all by itself. He wasn't sure when being a loner had started coming naturally, but that's the way he was now.

Moments later Lani walked up, a menu in her hand. "Hi."

He nodded. "How's it going?"

"That depends. In the last two days, more than one person has said they heard that you and I went out to dinner."

"But we didn't," he pointed out.

"I know and you know. But that's what we told Jordyn Leigh. Apparently, the Rust Creek Falls rumor mill is firing on all cylinders."

"Does it ever not?"

She thought for a moment. "When the power was out after the flood a couple years ago, it slowed down a lot because we didn't have phone service—cell or landline.

Other than that it always performs equal to or better than our expectations."

"So, folks in town think we're..."

"Dating." Her brown eyes were wary, waiting for a reaction.

A man could easily get caught up in those eyes, and Russ was trying his damnedest not to. But this temporary assignment required him to talk to her and word on the street was that they were going out, meaning he was interested. Just because he wasn't happy about that, it didn't make the conclusion wrong.

He studied her. "You don't look upset. Why is that?"

"We don't have to be covert about talking to each other. We can share information, and everyone will just think you're courting me."

"Do I look like the kind of guy who courts?" But he couldn't help smiling. She came out with some of the darnedest things, and it was getting harder to overlook the way her sunshine lit up the darkest corners of his soul.

"Call it what you want," she said. "Courting. Flirting. Set your cap for. Woo. Cozy up to. *Date.* I'm your ticket to not being an outsider. If people think you've got the hots for me, they'll let down their guard with you."

There was no *thinking* about it. He definitely had the hots for her. He'd proved that in a jail cell because he couldn't seem to help himself. And he hadn't been able to forget about her since. But she was right.

"Okay, then," he said. "Let's do something that will set the town rumor mill on fire."

Russ settled his hands on her hips and moved her between his legs. Those big brown eyes went wide with surprise, and her mouth formed an O. He just didn't have the reserves of willpower to keep himself from kissing her, just a soft touch of his lips to hers. It was barely contact, but set him on fire just the same.

"Well, color me fuchsia," she said against his mouth. There was a hitch in her breathing. "One picture is worth a thousand gossip-filled phone calls."

"Roger that." His own breathing was more unsteady than he would have liked. And he hoped the four guys who'd flirted with her were watching. "But you're working. I don't want to get you fired and lose a potential information stream."

"Right." With what looked an awful lot like real reluctance, she moved away and used the menu still in her hand to fan herself. "Speaking of that, have you found out anything?"

There was no one close enough to them to overhear, what with the noise level on a busy night. He didn't think a short exchange was a problem now that everyone thought they had a good reason for chatting.

"I was hoping you had something," he said.

"No. Does that mean you don't, either?"

He linked his fingers with hers and set their joined hands on his thigh. Just to maintain their cover, of course. "I've talked to the couple who got married that day and hosted the reception, their family and friends. I interviewed Bob and Ellie Traub, parents of the groom, who mixed up the punch. Just fruit juice and mixers and a little sparkling wine, that's all. They gave me no reason to think they're not telling the truth about the harmless ingredients used in making it."

"So we're back to square one?"

"Looks that way. Unless you overheard something here."

"Nothing." Her eyes turned darker and more troubled. "I can't think of anyone who would do something like this."

Her hand was starting to feel too natural in his, too good. He removed his fingers from hers and folded his arms over his chest. "My list of suspects hasn't changed."

She searched his face and came to a conclusion that made her mouth thin to a grim line. "And I'm on it."

The betrayal in her voice made him feel as if he'd kicked a kitten. He didn't like the feeling, and it brought out his defensive streak.

"Look at it from my point of view," he said. "I still don't know why you deliberately stole my keys to the jail cell and kept me locked up. Are you an accomplice? Working with someone else to keep the law busy? If I'd been out there where I should have been, maybe I'd have seen something, and whoever did this would be off the streets."

"We'll never know," she said, as the sparkle in her eyes flickered and went dark. "You have no reason to believe me, but I didn't do anything to the punch and I have no idea who did. For what it's worth, I do understand why you're skeptical about me."

"Generous of you." Russ hated that doubt about anyone he met was his go-to emotion now. It might be an asset for law enforcement but not the rest of his life. He'd never regretted it more than he did right this second. "But here's the thing that keeps tripping me up. Detective work is logical, and with you things just don't add up. It's that simple. If you want to come clean, that could change my mind."

She caught her bottom lip between her teeth then shook her head. "You have no idea how much I wish I could, but I made a promise. I have to honor that."

So she did have an ulterior motive, and it was about someone else. Under normal circumstances her loyalty might have impressed him, but nothing about this was ordinary. Someone had endangered people in this town, and he'd been hired to find out who. He had a promise to honor, too. From where he was sitting this looked an awful lot like a stalemate.

"I'll take that menu now," he said. "And could I get a beer?"

"Coming right up." It obviously wasn't easy, but she gave him a flirty smile.

Russ realized that she was pretty good at pretending. Although there was no denying the sparks between them. But he had to be skeptical of her motives and the sparks between them that refused to go away.

Lani returned and put a cocktail napkin on the scarred bar then set a bottle of beer on it. She smiled brightly, but the expression didn't match her words. "I really don't understand how you can use me in this investigation and still believe that I might be responsible for doing that to my friends and neighbors. My family was there, too."

Before he could tell her she had a point, she walked away. But that saying about keeping your friends close and your enemies closer kept running through his mind. Still, there was a part of him that didn't buy Lani Dalton as an enemy. He trusted Gage Christensen, and the man had urged Russ to use her as a reliable source.

In spite of his respect for Gage, he held tight to his skepticism. Russ had a sneaking suspicion that his doubts about Lani were all that stood between him and breaking his promise not to let another woman make a fool of him.

"Thanks for inviting me to dinner." Russ was sitting in the backyard at Gage Christensen's ranch house, not far from the heart of town.

"No problem," the sheriff answered. "Consider this a celebration for getting through the long Labor Day weekend without a repeat of the crisis on the Fourth of July."

"Definitely something to drink to." They clinked the long necks of their beer bottles.

Russ was enjoying this and the mild September air at the same time he was missing the friendly atmosphere of the Ace in the Hole. Or maybe the feeling was more about going three days without seeing the pretty brown-eyed brunette who worked there. But the last time he'd talked to her, she'd been pretty ticked off at him. Hell, he couldn't blame her. If someone accused him of getting the whole town drunk, he'd be mad, too.

The sun had just slipped past the mountains, and the yard was bathed in shade. On the patio, four Adirondack chairs with thick cushions formed a conversation area with a round table in the center. Gage had ribs and chicken in the smoker and his wife, Lissa, had set out appetizers: cheese, crackers, toasted French bread and some creamy vegetable dip.

"Eat up, Russ." After arranging everything on the table to her satisfaction, Lissa sat down beside him. She was a beautiful blue-eyed redhead, outgoing and friendly.

Russ put down his beer and took one of the small plates she'd set out. "If my appetite is spoiled, I'm blaming you."

"I'll send you home with leftovers if you can't eat dinner."

"You do know I'm staying at Strickland's Boarding House and there are no room refrigerators?"

"Then you'll just have to clean your plate. We thought it was time to have you over for a home-cooked meal. Right, Gage?"

"Right." The sheriff pointed to his wife and mouthed, *it was her idea.* Then he put the lid back on the smoker and joined them. "Lissa was worried about you being a lonely bachelor."

"*Worried* is a little strong." She picked up her glass of white wine and sipped. "But you uprooted your life to try to figure out who committed a crime here in our town. The least we can do is make you feel at home just a little."

Russ almost wished the couple had just let him be. Not that he didn't appreciate the gesture. They were friendly and entertaining, and the smells coming from that smoker made his mouth water. But from the second Lissa had opened the door and settled him out here on the patio, a feeling of dissatisfaction bordering on emptiness spread through him. Feminine touches were everywhere, from flowers and pictures to pillows and a hanging rack in the kitchen for pots and pans. This place felt like wedded-bliss central, and he envied these two people. If anything, being here made him feel more like a lonely bachelor than bunking at the boardinghouse. It was like being on the outside looking in.

"Speaking of feeling at home..." He looked at Lissa. "How do you like living in Rust Creek Falls after living in the city?"

"It's different," she said.

Following the flood that nearly destroyed Rust Creek Falls, she'd come here representing an organization called Bootstraps. Her mission was to help people rebuild their lives after losing homes and businesses. While she'd worked with Gage coordinating relief efforts, the two had fallen in love.

Russ had gone to Denver and understood how different a small town and big city were. None of his reasons for coming back to Montana were positive. That made him wonder about Lissa's response.

"Define *different*," he said.

"It's a slower pace. A lot less stress. People know your business." She sipped her wine, a thoughtful look on her face. "But I saw firsthand how everyone pulled together and helped each other. I love this place, where a person can count on their neighbors when the chips are down." She smiled and held out her hand to her husband, who was sitting beside her. When he took it and squeezed her fingers she said, "Plus, then I fell in love with this man. That sealed the deal for me because he wouldn't live anywhere else. And I couldn't live without him."

An image popped into Russ's mind of Lani, lying in his arms with her hair a mess and her dress all wrinkled. But she still managed to look more beautiful than any woman he'd ever met. That night, locked in the jail cell, she'd said almost the same thing about this town.

Russ looked at his friend. "What do you love about this place, Gage?"

"I have the best of all possible worlds." The sheriff, a muscular guy with brown hair and eyes, shifted in his chair. "There's this little piece of land that's mine. I have a few cattle and horses. And I really like being the sheriff of Rust Creek Falls. Helping folks and making sure everything in town runs like a well-oiled machine is satisfying in a way that I can't even put into words."

"Balance," Russ said.

"Exactly. And when something isn't in balance it bothers me." He sipped from his bottle of beer. "That's why I really want to know how and why so many people who are normally solid and steady ended up acting so out of their heads at that wedding. It's my responsibility to make sure it doesn't happen again."

"*Our* job," Russ said.

"Is there anything new on the investigation?" Lissa asked.

"Not yet. Everyone I talked to claims to have seen nothing. Although even if they had, most of them were in no condition to remember anything useful."

"There's at least one person who remembers an awful lot of details," Lissa commented.

"The gossip columnist," Russ said.

"Right." Lissa looked at each of them. "The person who writes the pieces in Sunday's edition of the *Rust Creek Falls Gazette* seems to have a whole lot of details from that night."

"How much confidence do you have in gossip?" Russ had read the back issues but wondered what the sheriff's wife thought.

"Well, I can't say that anything was a lie. Will and Jordyn Leigh *did* get married suddenly."

"But they're in love." When both of them gave him funny looks Russ said, "I talked to her, and she admitted that the effects of the punch lowered their inhibitions, but it all worked out and they're glad to have found each other."

Lissa nodded. "It's also true that Levi and Claire Wyatt had a falling-out that night. But their relationship seems stronger now that differences have been aired out so publicly. That happened because of being under the influence of whatever was in that punch." She snapped her fingers. "And don't forget that poker game where Brad Crawford won Old Man Sullivan's ranch. So whoever wrote those columns saw things."

"And I would give anything to know the identity of that person." Russ set his empty appetizer plate on the table and grabbed his beer bottle. "So, Lissa, any idea who's writing Rust Creek Ramblings?"

"How would I know?" Her blue eyes were blank for several moments then sparkled with humor when she caught his drift. "Because I'm a blogger you think I might have some psychic connection with another writer?"

"Long shot," he admitted. "But worth a try."

"I know it's a guilty pleasure, but I can't wait for the Sunday paper. Reading that column to find out what's going on with people is just too much fun."

"Whatever floats your boat." Russ shrugged.

"It does. And speaking of that..." Her eyes sparkled in a way that made him nervous. "I'm curious about something that wasn't in the paper."

"What?" Russ asked warily.

"You arrested Lani Dalton that night." She glanced at her husband. "And I have a reliable source who says the two of you were locked up together for a few hours."

"Really?" He looked at the sheriff.

"Sorry." Gage didn't look sorry. "She has her ways."

"I do." Lissa gave Russ her I'll-get-it-out-of-you look. "And I would really like to know what the two of you did to occupy yourselves for so long in jail."

He shrugged. "Oh, you know…"

She tilted her head and gave him a pitying look. "You seriously believe that's going to get you off the hook with me?"

"A guy can hope." When she shook her head, Russ sighed. Wild horses couldn't drag the whole truth out of him, but he could throw her a bone. "Okay. You win."

"And don't forget it. Now spill your secrets, Detective."

"Lani and I talked." At her look he added, "It was her idea."

"Now, there's a big surprise." Her tone was wry. "No one would accuse you of talking their ear off of your own free will."

"It's part of my charm." When Lissa laughed he thought his distraction had worked.

"So you expect me to believe you spent *hours* alone with a pretty girl like Lani and nothing happened besides conversation?"

"Like what?" He gave his friend a help-me-out-here look.

Gage stood and headed for the smoker. "I'm going to check the ribs."

Whatever happened to male solidarity? Russ wondered. Apparently, things changed when a man got married.

"Did you kiss her?" Lissa asked.

That was a loaded question, and he knew where it would lead. Russ decided on a flanking maneuver. "Did Gage tell you that she stole the keys to the cell to keep me locked in?"

"He did. What's your point?"

"People with nothing to hide, who have done nothing

wrong, don't do things like that." He shifted in his chair. "That means she can't be ruled out as a suspect."

"Lani Dalton? Seriously?" Lissa shook her head and looked at her husband, who had rejoined them. "What do you think?"

"I've known that girl and her family all my life. She's open, honest, loyal. Never been in trouble. If she's guilty, I'd take a dip in Badger Creek in the dead of winter."

"I'd like pictures of that," his wife teased.

"There won't be any because there's no way Lani did anything to that punch," Gage said emphatically.

Russ wanted to believe him but refused to let go of his doubts. Maybe that was an overabundance of caution, but he tended to think it was more about keeping her at a distance. Letting down his guard was the first step in trusting, and he wouldn't do that again.

Chapter Seven

After riding fences all day, Lani watched the sun sink lower in the sky as she headed back to Anderson's house on the Dalton ranch compound. She was hungry, dirty and tired, really looking forward to getting home to her parents' house in town for a hot shower and her mother's meatloaf. She rode into the barn and dismounted then led Valentino over to the water trough for a drink. She gave him a good rubdown and a generous portion of oats before walking to the house to see Anderson.

But as soon as she saw the familiar truck parked out front beside her own, it was clear that her plan for a hot shower and dinner was going to have to wait.

"Damn it, Russ," she muttered. "You better not be here to arrest Anderson."

Or accuse him of doctoring the punch. She was still annoyed about the other night when he'd insinuated she'd been responsible for getting the whole town drunk. The funny thing was that she didn't get the feeling his heart was all in on suspecting her. It was only after kissing her in front of everyone at the Ace in the Hole that he brought up the suspect list then aired his doubts about her. As if he was reinforcing his reasons for pushing her away. But everyone was a suspect, and the investigation could be the reason he was here at the ranch. She needed to find out what was going on.

She walked inside without knocking and found her brothers in the living room with the detective. His back was to her and she couldn't see his expression, but that body language didn't say relaxed.

"He threw the first punch when Travis wasn't looking, so I stepped in," Anderson was calmly explaining. "Skip Webster is a jealous hothead. Anyone in town will confirm that if you ask them."

Lani had slammed the door, and the wood floor didn't muffle the noise from her boots. It appeared no one had heard her come in, and she chalked that up to a surplus of testosterone making these three men deaf.

She didn't wait to be asked. "Skip Webster *is* a jealous hothead. That's exactly what went through my mind when I saw what happened."

At the sound of her voice, Russ turned. "Hi, Lani."

"Detective." She met his gaze, trying to decipher what was in his. She couldn't and decided she didn't much like the cop face that hid what he was thinking. "What brings you out here?"

"As I was just explaining to your brothers, I'm investigating all of the incidents that occurred after the Traub-MacCallum wedding. And that the sheriff and I believe the only reasonable explanation for why folks who are normally easygoing and law-abiding started acting crazy after drinking the punch is that it was spiked."

"What does that have to do with my brothers?" She walked past him to stand with Anderson and Travis. Her body language was telling Russ that this was three against one if he was going after Anderson for assault and battery when it so obviously had been self-defense.

"It's okay, Lani. No need for you to get involved," Anderson said. *Any more than you already are*, his look told her.

"I'm not here to single anyone out." Russ rubbed a hand across the back of his neck. "I'm interviewing everyone who was in the park that day, which is pretty much the whole town. Someone I spoke to remembered Travis and Anderson being there because of the altercation."

"It was stupid what happened," Anderson said. "Although that's just an impression, since the whole thing is kind of hazy. And you're right about people being rowdy, but Skip Webster throwing a punch is pretty much how he operates on a routine basis. He never pressed charges, by the way."

"I know."

Lani felt the heat and sharp accusation in Russ's hazel eyes when he looked at her. She knew he was thinking about being locked up that night instead of arresting her brother. He wouldn't forgive her for taking his keys, so it probably wasn't wise to point out that she'd saved him a pile of paperwork. Not to mention rescuing an indeterminate number of trees. The goal had been to keep her brother out of jail. Whatever was in that punch had given her the guts to do what she had to. And she was sworn to secrecy about her motive.

"Have you made any progress on the case?" she asked.

"None. I was just getting to that when you came in." His eyes narrowed first on Travis then Anderson. "Did either of you see or hear anything suspicious that night?"

"Besides the fact that you arrested my sister?" Travis said.

Lani felt Anderson tense and wished Travis hadn't

brought that up. She couldn't explain because it would lead to more questions she wasn't at liberty to answer. She had to do damage control.

"Like Russ said—" she met his gaze "—along with everyone else, I was acting weird, and it was getting pretty disorderly."

"I arrested her because she was going to hurt herself in that fountain. So I took her in for her own protection."

"He was there to maintain the peace," she confirmed.

"Maintaining the peace must have been a challenge when you were locked up in a jail cell with my sister." Travis had the angry, defensive big-brother thing down to a T.

Lani loved him for it, but barreling down this road wouldn't do Anderson any favors. "If it's all the same to you, Travis, that wasn't my finest hour, and I'd rather not talk about it. Except to say the whole thing was my fault, not Russ's."

The detective looked surprised that she'd backed him up. It bothered her that he would never know she had a good reason for doing the wrong thing.

Russ looked at her brothers. "The sheriff and I figure someone spiked the punch, and the subsequent individual behavior is a direct result of that illegal act, so no one will be held accountable. We're only interested in finding out who's responsible for drugging everyone and why."

"So it doesn't happen again, right, Detective?" she clarified.

"Exactly." He looked at her, and his eyes went smoky hot for a second before he shuttered the emotions.

"I'm not buying it." Travis still looked angry. "He's got a funny way of asking a question, making it sound more like an accusation."

"Easy, Trav—" Anderson put a steadying hand on his brother's arm. "I don't like it any more than you do, but he's the law."

It was so like Anderson to be the voice of reason, calming everyone around him. Now that she thought about it, Russ did the same thing. Maybe it had something to do with being the oldest sibling.

"He doesn't work for the Rust Creek Falls Sheriff's Department." Travis's gaze was full of suspicion. "Kalispell is his jurisdiction. And from what I hear, he's there because he couldn't hack it when he was with the Denver Police Department."

Lani was looking at Russ and saw the muscle jerk in his jaw. Clearly there was a story there, and she would give anything to hear what happened because it had obviously changed him—and she wanted to know everything about it. But this wasn't the time or place to discuss the matter.

"Look, you guys," she said to her brothers. "Maybe you've been spending too much time on the ranch, but here's the scoop. The sheriff hired Russ to investigate, and he's taken time from his life to do that. The least we can do is cooperate in order to get to the bottom of what happened."

"Be that as it may, he's an outsider," Travis commented. "If Gage Christensen asked me anything, I'd be happy to answer."

"That's the thing." Lani glanced up at her brother then back to Russ. "He's standing in for Gage, and we have an obligation to help. The fact that he isn't from around here makes him perfect for this. His objectivity won't be in question because he has no emotional investment in the outcome of the investigation."

Although Lani was wishing more and more that he had an emotional investment in *her*. She'd tried to stay mad at him for refusing to cross her off the suspect list. But as soon as she'd seen him here standing up to her brothers, her anger deserted her. And she really missed it.

"I heard that you're going out with him." Travis angled

his head toward Russ then gave her a challenging look. "What's up with that?"

It was too much to hope that gossip regarding their public kiss at the bar wouldn't get to her brothers. Normally, they didn't meddle in her relationships, but being questioned about that day in the park had pushed Travis's buttons.

"It's not serious. Russ and I are just getting to know each other," she said.

"That's right," he confirmed, but something flickered in his eyes.

"Are you sure about this?" Travis asked. "About him?"

"No one gets a guarantee about a person," she snapped. "That's why it's called becoming acquainted. And really, it's no one's business but mine."

"Understood," her brother said, but there was disapproval in the dark stare he leveled at her.

"Look, I'm only asking questions." Russ faced the other two men squarely, feet braced wide, looking them straight in the eyes. "Even though your memories of the night in question aren't clear, you might know something and not even realize it."

"You're asking if we saw anyone suspicious hanging around," Anderson guessed.

"Pretty much," Russ agreed.

"Look." Travis's voice had less of an edge, but the sarcasm was ratcheted up. "Everyone in town was at the reception. Everyone was getting something to drink. It was a hot day."

"Was there anyone you didn't recognize? A stranger? Someone who looked suspicious? Anything out of the ordinary?"

The two brothers looked at each other, clearly trying to remember, then shook their heads. Anderson spoke for both of them. “Community events are held in that park all the time, and I didn’t see anything different about this one.”

“Okay. I appreciate your help.” Russ nodded.

“Are we done here?” Travis asked.

“For now.” Russ glanced at each of them.

“Okay,” Lani said. “I’ll see you out. I’m heading back to town.” She looked at Travis, who’d driven his own truck to work today from their parents’ house. “See you at home. Bye, Anderson. See you in the morning.”

“Drive carefully,” he said.

She nodded then headed to the door with Russ behind her, certain that his gaze was on her back. Now that the tension was gone, she thought about her appearance. Spending the day on horseback didn’t lend itself to looking cover-girl gorgeous. She was dusty and sweaty, and if she took off her Stetson there would be serious hat hair. Not to mention no makeup and grime all over her face. He was probably thanking his lucky stars that they weren’t actually dating.

Walking down the porch steps, she felt the need to say something. “Travis and Anderson aren’t normally so prickly.”

“I didn’t think they were.” His expression was cop face again.

“No one is at their best when being questioned about a crime.”

Duh. He already knew that better than she ever could. She’d defended him to her brothers and was now doing the same for her brothers. For reasons she didn’t quite get, it was important that Russ didn’t think the worst of her family.

“My brothers are good men. Not perfect. They have flaws, but would never do anything dishonorable.”

“I get that, Lani.” He walked over to her truck and

opened the driver's-side door. "I'll follow you back to town."

"Okay. Thanks." Lani wasn't ready to say goodbye, but after she climbed in he closed the door, indicating that he wanted to be done. "See you."

"Right." He turned his back and walked to his truck.

If he hadn't cut this short, she knew she would have babbled on and defended herself. Told him again that she wasn't in the habit of throwing herself at handsome cops in a jail cell, but he didn't give her the chance. All business, all the time for Detective Russ Campbell.

That was probably for the best, she told herself. Otherwise he might confirm that the intimate moment they'd shared in that jail cell meant nothing to him.

"Lani, I need to talk to you."

Starting a conversation like that never meant anything good, Lani thought. She hadn't even closed the front door before hearing her father's voice from the kitchen. When Ben Dalton was waiting for her, she knew her shower and dinner were going to have to wait a little longer.

"Hi, Dad." She walked into the room, and the good smells coming from the oven made her stomach growl. "Where's Mom?"

"She had to run to Crawford's. Something about making gravy."

"Mmm." She was barely back in control after seeing Russ at the ranch, and now this. What the heck was going on? The last time her father said he needed to talk to her she'd been a teenager, and he took away her cell phone until her geometry grade improved. "What's up, Dad?"

Her father was a tall man, about six foot two, with some silver running through his brown hair. It was a family joke that his kids had turned him gray. And he was looking so serious right now, it was a wonder his hair didn't turn white on the spot. The man had no belly fat and didn't make a habit of imbibing, so it was a surprise when he pulled a beer out of the refrigerator, twisted the cap off and took a long swallow. Good Lord, she'd driven him to drink!

He set the longneck bottle on the granite-topped island beside him. "Anderson just called."

"Oh?" She figured it had something to do with Russ's visit, but as a lawyer's daughter she'd learned not to say much before knowing the full scope of the situation.

"He said Detective Campbell was at the ranch asking questions about a fight at the July Fourth wedding."

"That's true."

"Did you know that Anderson decked Skip Webster that day?" Ben was wearing a white dress shirt with sleeves rolled up and his red tie loosened, not the way he would appear in court. But that authoritative voice firing the question made it feel as if she was in the witness box with judge and jury looking on.

In her mind she heard the words: swear to tell the truth, the whole truth and nothing but the truth. So help you God.

"I'm waiting, Lani."

"Yes, sir. I knew Anderson hit Skip. For the record, the jerk had it coming. He threw a punch, the first one, at Travis. When he wasn't looking. Anderson did what he had to do."

"You saw what happened?"

"Yes."

Ben took another pull on his beer. "I'd heard that Gage Christensen hired Detective Campbell to find out why everyone went off the rails that night."

"I heard that, too." Because Russ had told her himself.

"It's a good idea. And folks will rest easier knowing that something is being done." But her father was frowning. "I just never expected my family to be accused of spiking that punch."

"Russ wasn't accusing, just asking questions, Dad. Gathering information. It put Travis on the defensive. You of all people should know that Russ can't play favorites if he's going to get to the bottom of this."

"I do know. That doesn't mean I like it." He toyed with the bottle sitting on the island, turning it in his fingers.

"He's talking to everyone who was in the park that night." She leaned her back against the cupboards across from him and folded her arms over her breasts.

"Have you spoken with Detective Campbell about this before today?"

"I was the first one questioned." Possibly because of her behavior in the jail cell that night.

"Why?"

What she did wasn't something she could share with her father. "Because Gage told him that my access to the public could be useful, and Russ must have agreed."

"Why?" her father asked again.

She wished it was because he liked, respected and wanted her with an intensity that burned bright and hot but that wasn't the case.

"Why not start with me?" she said instead. "It's as good a place as any, what with the flow of customers in and out of the Ace in the Hole on any given day. People tend to say too much when they're drinking. I might have inadvertently come across information to help him in the investigation."

"Did you?"

"No."

"I don't mind telling you that I'm very concerned, Lani." Her father's expression was grave.

"I can see why. In a town that prides itself on community and fellowship, it would be a shame to cancel public celebrations because of what happened."

"That's true. But I actually meant that I'm concerned about you."

Back to not embellishing at the risk of giving away something she didn't intend to. "Oh?"

"I know what you're doing." Her father's look was wry. "I taught you."

"What?"

"Answer everything with a one-word question when you're trying to hide something."

"Why would I?" That was a three-word answer. "I have nothing to hide." Liar, liar, pants on fire. If there was a deception buzzer, it would have sounded just then.

"Okay." Her dad looked at the floor for several moments then met her gaze. "Then tell me this. Why did Russ Campbell arrest you that night?"

"You know why. All of Rust Creek Falls knows why. It was in the *Gazette*, in that gossip column."

"Tell me again." He was in full lawyer mode now.

"I drank the punch. Along with everyone else, I was completely unaware that it was spiked and made me drunk and do things I wouldn't ordinarily do. I jumped into the fountain at the park. It was hot and the water was refreshing."

Some of the heat she'd experienced was less about summer weather and more about her close proximity to Russ Campbell. Again, not something she planned to share with her father, of all people!

"I think there's more to it than that." He gave her the dad stare, which intensified exponentially when he threw in some attorney-on-the-attack technique. "If I have the timeline right, Anderson was involved in that altercation just before you took your act into the water."

"So?"

"Really?" He looked at her. "That's not going to work."

"I object."

"You don't get to. This isn't a court of law. But points for trying." His grin was fleeting.

"I'm not sure what you want me to say, Dad."

"The truth would be good." He dragged his fingers through his hair. "You're involved in something."

"What do you mean?" A four-word response. Proof that he was gaining the upper hand.

Their father was an exceptional lawyer; Anderson should let him help with his legal problem. But they'd gone over that and he refused then swore her to secrecy. She'd never realized how truly awful it was to be caught in the middle.

"What I mean is that Anderson told me," her father said.

This was where she couldn't afford to get trapped and involuntarily spill something. "What did he tell you?"

"He said Detective Campbell was going to arrest him for assaulting Skip, and you created a diversion in the fountain."

"He told you that when he called a little bit ago?"

Her father shook his head. "It was a day or two after the fact."

"Then why are you asking me about it now?"

"Because now there's a police investigation into the park incident that endangered folks who unknowingly got drunk. And you were arrested during that incident. This has taken a serious turn. A detective is asking questions, and if I'm going to protect my kids, I need to know the truth."

"You know it already, Dad. Like Anderson said, I created a distraction to keep him from being arrested."

Lani knew her father was only trying to help, but the truth she'd been entrusted with weighed heavily on her. That put a defensive note in her voice. This interrogation was headed to a place where she'd have to draw a line in the sand, and she hated doing that. Ben Dalton was the most honest and loyal man she knew, and he set a high bar for his children. She looked up to him and tried to be like him. By that standard, she needed to guard the secret entrusted to her.

"What I don't understand is why you got involved. Anderson can take care of himself."

Not this time, she wanted to say. Her big brother had always been there for her. Taught her how to drive; and when she dinged the bumper of his new truck, instead of yelling at her, he made her get back in and drive it until her confidence was restored. When Lani and a couple friends toilet-papered the house of a popular boy who bullied some of the weaker kids, her brother took the blame to keep her from a grounding that would've made her miss the Homecoming dance. He was like their father, loyal and strong. And she wanted to be that for him.

She met her father's gaze without flinching. "He was protecting Travis, and I protected him. It's what Daltons do."

"I know." But her father was looking at her as if he could see into her soul.

She really hoped he couldn't because she would never willingly betray Anderson's trust.

"The problem is," he continued, "Russ Campbell spent some time locked in that cell along with you. That was also in Rust Creek Ramblings. I know it's gossip and so left it alone. Until now. But as I said, things have taken a turn, and we have more questions than answers."

"I know, Daddy." The worried look in his eyes made her move closer and put her arms around him. She pulled back and met his gaze, willing him to understand and not judge even though she couldn't give him all the facts. "I can only say that I had a very good reason for spending the night in jail. Fortunately, there were no legal consequences. Besides, in my own defense it has to be said that I was a victim of the spiked punch, too."

"Yes, but you made the conscious choice to intervene for your brother."

"I did. And you're not going to like this, but I can't tell you why."

"You're right. I don't like it." Was it a trick of the overhead lighting, or did he have more gray hair than a few minutes ago?

"I won't say I've never given you reason to worry," she started.

"Good. Because I'd take issue if you did." He smiled. "A father will always worry most about his daughters. It's part of the job description."

"Let me rephrase. I can say that I've never given you reason not to trust me."

He nodded. "That's the truth. You're a good girl."

"You and Mom taught us to put family first. I'm asking you to keep trusting me without all the facts. I know what I'm doing, Dad."

He studied her for a long moment and finally nodded. "Okay."

She kissed his cheek. "I'm going to take a long, hot shower."

"Good. I was going to say something—" The teasing expression was back on his face and, knowing him, that wasn't easy to pull off.

Lani headed upstairs feeling both better and worse. It was technically true that there were no legal consequences from her actions that night. But the personal ones were unsettling and ongoing. She hated that she was keeping the truth from the best parents on the planet, but awed that they trusted her in spite of it.

If only Detective Dreamy would give her the benefit

of the doubt. Even the sheriff vouched for her, but Russ refused to be swayed.

Maybe skepticism was a by-product of being a cop. Or the reason was something more personal. Something that caused him to leave Denver and come back to Montana.

It was time to find out which.

Chapter Eight

Russ had Lani's cell number on speed dial and had been fighting the urge to use it. Two days ago she'd defended him to her brothers, and he didn't know what to make of that. And her.

Now it was Sunday. He'd been working seven days a week since starting the investigation, and Gage insisted he take the day off and clear his head. Now the prospect of a very long day stretched in front of him.

And before he could stop himself, Russ hit the call button. Now he'd done it. Maybe she wouldn't pick up.

"Hello?"

And there was the sugar-and-spice-with-a-splash-of-sexy voice that took his breath away. "Hi, Lani."

"Russ. What's up?"

Damned if he knew, but now he was on the spot. "I know Friday and Saturday are busy at the bar. Just wondered if you've heard anything."

"Not so far."

He looked around the room he'd been renting at Strickland's Boarding House. It was neat as a pin and lonely as a space walk. The bed was covered by a quilted spread without a single wrinkle, and that made him think about twisted sheets and tangled legs. The problem with hearing her voice was that it gave him a powerful need to see her.

"Maybe it's time to shake up the investigation," he suggested.

"How?"

"Good question." He blew out a long breath. "Maybe we should get together and brainstorm."

"Well, I—"

"You've got plans." The depth of his disappointment was surprising. "Another time."

"Not so fast. The thing is, my mom cooks dinner for the family every Sunday, and expects us all to be there. Very few excuses get sanctioned. I'll have to figure out what to tell her."

"You're not planning to say anything about being involved in the investigation?" He didn't like the idea of not having that excuse to see her.

"Of course not. I just meant it's important for me to come up with an acceptable reason for not being here. Since I'm not bleeding, on fire or just had a baby, I need to get creative."

"What about meeting my family?"

"Well," she said thoughtfully, "they think we're going out, so it's a logical next step. As lies go it would probably work because one of the ironclad Dalton rules is family first."

"It wouldn't be a lie if we actually go to the farm." In for a penny, in for a pound, he thought. "I'll pick you up in an hour."

"Okay."

Russ didn't want it to be the truth, but suddenly his day off looked a whole lot more exciting.

It was late in the afternoon when Lani sat in the passenger seat of Russ's truck as he drove toward Boulder Junction, the small town halfway between Rust Creek Falls and Kalispell. Her parents happened to be together when she broke the news about not being there for Sunday dinner. She knew her dad told her mom everything, including the conversation they'd had after Russ interviewed her brothers. And she could see the curiosity in her parents' eyes, but they were on their best behavior when Russ came to the door to get her. There was no interrogation and she appreciated that they trusted her.

"Your parents are very nice." It was as if Russ was reading her mind.

"I know. And now they're very curious about us."

"Oh?"

"When I told them you were taking me to meet your family, I was questioned relentlessly about how serious we are."

His mouth curved up, but aviator sunglasses hid the expression in his eyes. "Then you've already had a preview of what to expect from my family. Just maintain your cover and follow my lead."

"Yes, sir. Understood, sir."

He laughed and she felt an unexpected sense of satisfaction because that didn't happen often. Sometimes being with him felt easy and natural, not an act. A peek into what it could be like if they hadn't started out on the wrong foot. Best not to think about what might have been and concentrate on what was happening now.

During the drive, Lani waited for him to bring up the investigation, but by the time they reached the Campbell farm he hadn't mentioned it. Just over a rise she could see a two-story yellow clapboard house with white trim. Behind it there was land as far as she could see, planted with different crops that formed a sort of natural patchwork.

Russ pulled into the curved drive and parked his truck in front of the house. Beyond it, down a dirt road, there were outbuildings that no doubt contained tools and equipment. She could see a green tractor and another huge machine. No idea what it did for a living. Trees shaded the house, and the grass in the yard was neatly trimmed. Shrubs and flowers lined the walkway up to the solid oak front door.

"This is very charming," she said.

"Yeah." He took off his sunglasses and set them on the dashboard. "Let's go get the interrogation over with, then I'll give you a tour of the place and we can talk about the case."

"Okay."

After exiting the vehicle, they walked up two steps to the front door, where Russ knocked. Moments later a pretty young woman answered.

"Hi, Addie."

"Russ." The green-eyed redhead grinned then gave him a big hug. "I didn't know you were coming."

"Surprise."

Addie looked at her, one auburn eyebrow lifting. "And who's this?"

"Lani Dalton. A friend." He put his hand at her waist, apparently remembering their cover. "Lani, this is my little sister, Adeline."

"Russell, you know I hate that name." She winced. "Addie will do."

Lani shook her hand. "It's lovely and old-fashioned."

"That's what Mom says and exactly what I don't like about it." She pulled the door wide. "She'll be happy to see you, big brother. And to meet your friend. Everyone is here for dinner. Don't be afraid, Lani."

"I've got three brothers and two sisters. I'm not easily intimidated." But now that they were actually here, she *was* a little nervous.

Just inside was a formal dining room where the large table was set for dinner. The wood-plank floor of the entry led to the kitchen with stainless-steel appliances, double ovens and cooktop. Very modern and not quite what Lani had pictured in a farmhouse. This place could be in a photo shoot for *Better Homes and Gardens* magazine.

"Look who's here," Addie announced.

A woman who looked to be in her fifties turned from stirring something. She had short, stylishly cut brown hair and hazel eyes. Russ's eyes. She smiled and, like her son, it transformed her appearance.

"You should have told me you were coming." She looked at Lani. "And that you were bringing someone."

Russ looked down at her. "Lani, this is my mother, Teresa Campbell. Mom, Lani Dalton."

"It's nice to meet you," Teresa said.

"Same here," Lani answered.

"Everyone come meet Russ's friend," his mom ordered.

Three men were standing in the spacious adjoining family room, their attention focused on a wall-mounted flat-screen TV and the football game that was on. They took one last glance then did as directed and walked into the kitchen.

Russ shook hands with all three then made introductions. "This is my father, John," he said, indicating the older man with dark, silver-streaked hair. "My brothers, Micah and Carson."

When he moved closer to shake her hand, she noticed Micah's expression was just this side of wary, and he had a limp. She couldn't help wondering about it. The twinkle in

Carson's brown eyes reminded her of Travis's mischievous streak, and she pegged him as the youngest of the boys.

"It's a pleasure to meet all of you." Lani smiled.

"Tell me you're staying for dinner. Both of you," Teresa said.

Lani looked at Russ, giving him a look that said it was time for him to take the lead. "I don't know—"

"It's been a long time since you were here for Sunday dinner, Russell James."

"Uh-oh," Lani said. "It's never good when your mom uses both names. When I hear Lani Elizabeth it makes me want to put myself in time-out."

Everyone laughed, including Russ, and the tension she'd sensed in him eased.

"Yeah, Mom, we can stay. I'd like that if it's not too much trouble," he said.

"Of course not. I always make too much food."

A little while later, after extra places had been set and drinks handed out, they were sitting around the dining room table, passing fried chicken, mashed potatoes, salad and corn. When plates were filled they started eating, and the interrogation commenced.

"So, how did you and Russ meet?" Teresa asked.

Lani probably would have choked if she'd been chewing food. She should have expected the question. Her bad. But now she had to wing it, no pun intended to the chicken.

"It was on the Fourth of July. There was a wedding reception going on in the park, and Russ was on duty." That was the truth, but not the whole truth.

"You all know I fill in when needed," he said. "Gage Christensen has been my friend for a long time, and he's the sheriff of Rust Creek Falls. With one deputy short, he asked for my help."

"Gage is a nice young man. I bet he's as glad to have you back from Colorado as we are," his mom said. "And it's about time you brought a young lady to Sunday dinner." She turned to Lani and whispered, "He's been lonely since things ended with Alexis."

Lani saw his mouth pull tight. She wanted to hear about this probably way more than he wanted to talk about it.

"That woman was a witch," Addie said. "Probably still is."

At the head of the table John was nodding. "You dodged a bullet there, son. And leaving Denver was probably a blessing in disguise. Colorado's loss is our gain."

Russ shifted in his chair. "Dad, I—"

"Aren't you conducting a special investigation in Rust Creek Falls?" Micah asked, bailing out his brother.

"Yeah." Russ sent him a grateful look.

Lani figured that level of gratitude over changing the subject meant Russ would rather take a sharp stick in the eye than talk about either of those subjects. That made her curious and even extra determined to find out the details, maybe discover what made Russ Campbell tick. But he was off and running with an explanation of spiked punch and small-town anxiety. This wasn't the time to question him.

After the table was cleared, dishes cleaned up and leftovers put away, Teresa suggested Russ take Lani for a walk—show her around the property—and he jumped at the chance. It might have been about being alone with her, but she figured he just wanted to steer clear of their references to his past.

Side by side they walked up the road leading to the outbuildings, and he showed her the equipment and machinery that made farming on such a large scale possible. He pointed out where the different crops were planted, but that was only what they could see from this vantage point. Not too far from the house he stopped beside Boulder Creek, a valuable water source for the farm.

It was also a pretty spot with spruce and pine trees on

either side. The water cheerfully gurgled over rocks, and Lani sighed as she took in the peaceful surroundings.

She had a feeling what she was about to say was just the opposite of peaceful, but she was compelled to ask anyway. "Who's Alexis, and why did you leave the Denver Police Department?"

A dark look slid into his eyes and a muscle tightened in his jaw.

"You don't beat around the bush, do you?"

"No point. I'd be lying if I said I wasn't curious." She stared at him. "So what brought you back to Montana?"

"Let's just call it irreconcilable differences."

"The reason most often given for a divorce and just as empty of personal details." She shook her head. "Come on, Russ. Something happened. What made you leave—"

He reached out a finger and traced it over her mouth, a smoldering look in his eyes. Before she could regroup and finish asking her question, his mouth was on hers. The contact was like a zap of electricity and just as effective in frying her thoughts. Heat poured through her, pooling in her belly. His arms came around her, snuggling her closer, pressing her breasts against his chest.

He threaded his fingers into her hair, cupping the back of her head, holding her still while his tongue caressed the inside of her mouth and dueled with hers. He kissed her for a long time, sweetly, tenderly, gently, thoroughly, completely messing up her head.

Finally, he pulled back and fortunately didn't remove his arms, because she was fairly certain her weak legs wouldn't support her weight. The only sounds were their ragged breathing mingled with the babbling stream rushing past them.

Lani blinked up at him, and rational thought slowly returned. "So… As a distraction technique, that was pretty effective."

The corner of his mouth curved up nearly to adorable territory. "Did it work?"

"I got the message, if that's what you're asking. You don't want to talk about it."

"Smart girl."

"At least this time you picked a decent setting to kiss me. This is leaps and bounds better than the Ace in the Hole or a jail cell."

"I aim to please."

"No, you don't." If only. "Your goal was to avoid opening up about your past."

"There's no point." It was a surprise that he didn't deny the accusation. He let her go and stared at the gurgling stream. "Water under the bridge."

"I get the feeling it's a dark and twisty story." She saw his mouth thin and held up a hand. "I won't push. Don't worry."

"I appreciate that."

"You're welcome."

It cost her a lot to hold back the questions. If she wasn't starting to care about him, she would have asked whatever she wanted and damn the consequences. But she was starting to care about him a lot and didn't want to rock the boat. At least not yet.

He'd lied to Lani.

Russ had kissed her because he couldn't resist. He hadn't done it to distract her from asking about his past, but couldn't argue that stopping the questions was a happy by-product of his actions.

It was now Friday night, almost a week since taking her to the farm. Every day they'd chatted on the phone to compare notes about the investigation, and he always managed to keep her on longer because she made him laugh.

He liked her. More than he wanted to.

For the weekend he was taking a break from the investigation and patrolling the annual carnival for Rust Creek Falls Elementary School. Traditionally, this fund-raiser was held soon after Labor Day, when classes started up again. This year was no different, although the mayor and town council had urged the sheriff to be more vigilant after what happened on the Fourth of July. This was another public gathering, and there would be food and drinks, which put everyone on edge.

So here he was in the park. He stopped by the infamous fountain where he and Lani first clashed and saw her not far away in the bake-sale booth. Stalls were lined up parallel with the parking lot and contained various games and activities designed to make money that would fund school supplies, computers and extracurricular programs.

Lani was wearing a red apron that said Rust Creek Falls Elementary School in white letters, and her hair was pulled back in a sassy ponytail. She took a bill then smiled and gave a woman a plastic bag containing sugar cookies. That smile went straight through him, cranking up the tension already coiled tightly inside him every time he saw her or thought about her.

Through everything that happened in Denver, his professionalism had never slipped, but it was now when all he could think about was kissing Lani Dalton. As much as he would like to trust her, he had to focus on rebuilding his career, making up for the time he'd lost. He couldn't afford a distraction, to blindly put his faith in another woman—especially a woman with a secret.

Checking his watch, he realized it was time to put his cop skills back to work, because he wasn't being paid to look at Lani. It was getting late, and tonight's activities were almost over. Only a few people were milling around, and most of them were shutting down the booths until tomorrow morning.

The food was closed up and secured. Most of it was prepackaged, making tampering difficult. Everything else was being supervised by the school principal. If anyone started acting weird, he would know who to question.

Lani was counting money and didn't notice him right away. When she glanced up, the automatic smile that normally came so easily to her disappeared.

"Hi," she said.

"Evening." He slid his fingertips into the pockets of his jeans. "Everything quiet?"

"If you mean has anyone spiked the cupcake icing, the answer is no."

Her voice was a little cool, and he could understand why. Taking her to meet his family sent a certain message, one he hadn't meant to send. Everyone had told him how much they liked her, but he wasn't after their approval. He didn't need it, since there wasn't now and never would be anything serious between him and Lani. But then he'd kissed her and claimed it was nothing more than a distraction. As mixed messages went that was a doozy.

"Good. Nothing out of the ordinary." He nodded. "After what happened on the Fourth, we can't be too careful."

"Do you really think it could happen again?"

"My gut says no, but until we find the creep who did it, there's no way to know for sure." Shadows lurked in her dark eyes and made Russ want to protect her from whoever had messed with the punch that July day. It was a given that guarding everyone in town was part of his job, but with Lani the feeling was very different. Intense. And more personal than he cared to admit. "Are you finished for the night?"

She nodded. "I just have to give this money to Carol Watson, the parent coordinator in charge of this whole thing."

Just then an attractive brunette walked up beside him.

"Hi, Russ. It's so reassuring to have a law enforcement presence."

"Carol." Russ had met her during a final logistics meeting for this fund-raiser. Like everyone else in town, she was nervous about any community event since the wedding. "Everything is quiet."

The woman nodded. "Lani, how was business?"

"Good. Almost everything sold out." She handed over a blue zippered cash bag.

"Excellent. I've got volunteers lined up for Saturday and Sunday to donate more baked goods. Fingers crossed that the volume of customers keeps up."

"I'm pretty sure it will," Lani said. "Takes more than a little spiked punch to scare off the people of this town. Traditionally, folks in Rust Creek Falls support their school."

"From your mouth to God's ear," Carol said. "What happened on the Fourth was shocking and could scare even our resilient citizens off."

"We've been spreading the word that the sheriff's office has an increased presence," Russ said. "Everything possible is being done to make sure this fund-raiser goes smoothly."

"I know. And your vigilance is appreciated." She smiled but it was tense around the edges. "Lani, thanks for pitching in."

"No problem," Lani said. "My sister Paige teaches at the school and can be very persuasive in encouraging Dalton family volunteerism."

"Still…thank you." She nodded at both of them. "Good night."

Russ watched Lani put the few remaining cookies, cupcakes and brownies into a pink bakery box before grabbing her purse. She looked at him. "Good night, Russ."

He wasn't ready to say good-night. "I'll walk you to your car."

"I left it at home. Didn't want to deprive a paying customer of a parking space, since my house isn't that far from here."

"Then I'll give you a ride home," he said.

"That's all right." She exited the rear of the booth and came around to where he was standing. "See you around."

"Just a second." He loosely curled his fingers around her upper arm to stop her. "You've been on your feet all night. Might feel good to sit."

"I'm used to standing."

The outdoor park lights illuminated her tight expression. "What's bugging you, Lani?"

"Other than someone who gets their kicks from watching a whole town get drunk? That's not enough for you?" Her mouth pulled tight. "That really bugs me. People were trying not to be, but they were on edge tonight. This is supposed to be a fun and carefree event. It wasn't, and that's frustrating. Even working together we can't figure out who did it."

Her clipped tone and the pinched look on her face were evidence that she'd been feeling the pressure of watching out for suspicious behavior. She wasn't used to that, and it had taken a toll. Gently, he took the bakery box out of her hands.

"I'm taking you home."

There was a moment of hesitation before she nodded. "Okay."

Side by side they walked across the grass to the parking lot, where his truck was one of the few vehicles left. Gage's cruiser was still there, so he knew his friend was on alert. He opened the door for Lani and waited until she'd climbed inside. Then he went around to the driver's side and deposited the box of baked goods on the rear seat before getting behind the wheel.

Russ could practically feel the waves of anxiety rolling through her. "Talk to me, Lani."

"Everything is different since that day," she said. "This carnival used to be fun for the kids and parents, but now it's a big headache." She glanced over at him. "How do I know I'm not selling a child a cupcake that will make them sick?"

There was no way to be sure, but he wouldn't tell her that. He put the key in the ignition, started the car and backed out of the space. Then he exited the lot and turned right toward her house.

"Every precaution has been taken," he said. "The sign-ups were completely controlled. Items delivered were checked off a master list. Nothing was accepted without being on that list. All of the names were run by Gage and the school's administrative staff. We know who baked what and can cross-reference if anyone reports a problem. No one would try anything because the odds of getting caught are pretty high."

"But it's not impossible."

"True." He thought for a moment. "But the incident with the punch was different. No one expected it. No one was prepared. Now we're watching. If there's a tainted batch of cupcakes, it would be small-scale and easy to identify who did it. No one would take the risk."

"That makes sense." She sighed. "But I hate this. One person is ruining things for everyone."

"Yeah."

"I can't believe our investigation hasn't turned up a darn thing. We're no closer to finding out the truth."

"Not yet." If she'd noticed that he used their investigation as an excuse to see her Sunday then never brought the subject up, she didn't mention it.

"I'm not so sure anymore."

It bothered him that her fundamental trust in the goodness of people was shaken, and he wanted badly to reassure her. "I've been a detective for a long time. You never know when you'll get a lead that will break a case wide-open."

"Maybe sometimes it's necessary to do something to make things break your way."

Russ didn't like the sound of that. "What does that mean?"

"It's time to shake things up and see what happens." Those words were laced with a whole lot of stubborn.

"Never underestimate the value of pounding the pavement and the interview process from a law enforcement perspective."

"That's not working for me," she said.

He pulled the truck to a stop in front of her house, and the overhead light went on when she opened the door. Determination was written all over her face, and he had a bad feeling. "Whatever you're planning to do…don't."

"Brad Crawford won Old Man Sullivan's ranch in a poker game that night. I believe you would call that motivation." She met his gaze. "I'm going to get Brad to ask me out on a date, and then I'll find out what he knows."

"No, Lani. It could be dangerous and—"

She slammed the door and hurried into the house, effectively cutting off his protest. Frustration rolled through him, and he hit the steering wheel with the flat of his palm. Pain radiated up his arm but also cut through his irritation and let in a dose of reality.

It wasn't his detective instincts that were objecting to her going out with Brad Crawford. He didn't want her alone with another guy.

He was jealous.

Chapter Nine

Lani refused to give in to the yearning to turn and look at Russ driving away. She walked into the house, closed the door behind her then leaned her forehead against it. It occurred to her that he might be jealous at the idea of her going out with Brad Crawford, then she realized that was crazy and possibly a little pathetic. Darn him anyway. She swore he wouldn't get to her, but somehow he always did. There was something about the confident way he walked, the cocky tilt of his head, that adorable smile—when he chose to use it.

Things with him changed direction so fast a girl had no idea where she stood. One minute he was kissing her senseless, the next he treated her as a suspect in his case.

"Lani?"

Her sister's voice came from the kitchen. Lindsay must be home for the weekend. Busy with her last semester of law school before she'd study for the bar exam, she didn't have a lot of time to spare, though she tried to get back home as often as possible. But this visit was unexpected, and Lani wondered what was up. She headed in that direction and found her sister opening a bottle of Chardonnay. There were two wineglasses sitting on the island.

"How did you know I needed this?" Lani asked.

"Mom said you were working the carnival." There was a "duh" in her sister's voice as she poured the wine. "And I couldn't help noticing that the very hot and sexy Detective Campbell dropped you off. Again."

Lani didn't want to talk about that. She just took the glass her sister handed over and said, "You know me too well, sis. Thanks."

"And you know me." She held her wineglass up. "Let's drink to sisters before men."

"Right on." They clinked glasses and sipped. Lani thought her sister looked troubled. "Everything okay?"

"Oh, you know how it is. Men suck."

"Barry didn't meet your expectations?"

Lindsay's expression was wry. "I have an expectation of fidelity when a man suggests we be exclusive. Apparently, his interpretation of being faithful was different." She sighed, and the miserable look was back. "I caught him with his secretary. On the desk."

"Ouch." Lani winced. "But seriously, could that be any more clichéd?"

"I know, right? Absolutely no creativity." Her sister toyed with the end of her ponytail. There was a frown in her blue eyes. "Except that what they were doing on that desk showed quite a bit of imagination—and passion that I never experienced with him."

Lani's heart hurt for her sister. She gave her a quick, hard hug. "You know, I could tell you he's not worth crying over. There's someone out there for you who's ten times the man Barry is. That he'll get what's coming to him. But I'm not going to."

"Really?" Lindsay's eyebrows rose.

"Nope. Not going to go there," she confirmed. "Instead, I say we get Anderson, Travis and Caleb to pay him a visit."

"That's like putting out a hit on him. If I'm going to be a lawyer and an officer of the court, I can't condone that kind of behavior." But she grinned, and her unhappiness faded for a few moments.

"But it's not a hit," Lani insisted. "If the three of them simply walk into his office, Barry will start to sweat. Our brothers don't have to do anything but stand there and look like the avengers they could be. They're a pretty imposing threesome."

"The plan does have a certain appeal." Thoughtfully, she tapped her lips then shook her head. "Going to that much trouble would make him think I care."

"You do," Lani reminded her.

"Sadly. But ignoring him will put a dent in that ego of his. That's where he's vulnerable." Lindsay looked fierce for a moment before her eyes turned dark and tragic. "We talked about plans for the future. I was going to join his law practice and help him take on high-profile property development. That's not going to happen now."

"Better to find out before jumping into the deep end of the pool." Lani was aware that her sister already knew that. She also knew that right this minute the truth of the statement wouldn't make Lindsay feel any better. Only time would do that. "You'll find someone, Linds."

"I used to believe that once upon a time. Naively, I used to have hope. Then I got cheated on. Not once. Not twice." She held up three fingers. "Third time's the charm."

"What does that mean?"

"Isn't it obvious? I give off some kind of vibe that makes men think they can cheat on me. Or—" if possible her expression grew even more bleak "—I'm just a placeholder. Someone to be used until a better prospect comes along."

Now Lani was getting worried. Her sister tended to look at life as not being fair. It was one of the reasons she'd wanted to be an attorney, to sort of even the odds for folks who didn't have faith. But this hopeless attitude seemed deeply entrenched and reinforced, a core belief that would be difficult to shake.

It was time for some tough love, and that meant not playing her game. "That's just ridiculous. You're a hot, beautiful woman who has a lot to offer. In high school you were voted the girl most likely to break men's hearts."

"That's when the curse began," she countered, her voice full of conviction.

"Oh, please. Don't be a martyr. This isn't about you. There's nothing wrong with you except for your judgment in men. Try swearing off them for a while. Clear your head. A different perspective and all that."

"You're onto something, sis." Lindsay drained the rest of the wine in her glass. "I'm done with men and not temporarily, either. This is permanent."

"That's the spirit." No point in trying to change her mind right now when the wound was still raw and bleeding, Lani thought.

"They'll call me the bachelorette barrister. Don't you just love alliteration?"

"It has a certain ring." A little reverse psychology. "Maybe we should spin off a group from the Newcomers Club and call it the Wallflowers Club."

"It should be singular, since I would be the only member."

"I'm joining with you," Lani explained.

"You can't. What would Detective Dreamy say?"

"He doesn't get to say anything about what I do." Lani meant the words even though part of her wanted him to have a say.

"That's not the way I see it." Lindsay rested her elbows on the island countertop.

"Then it's time to get your eyes checked because that's the way it is."

"You're seriously trying to convince me that you don't have feelings for Russ Campbell?" her sister asked.

"Oh, I have feelings all right, but not what you're implying."

"So nothing has changed between the two of you since the Fourth of July when you gave the impression that he was one step up from a Neanderthal?"

"You could say that." Lani wouldn't say it but didn't mind if her sister put the thought out there.

"Then I rest my case."

"Good." She hated that her sister was a lawyer. It was like talking to their father, being cross-examined, every little thing she said analyzed and dissected.

Lindsay pointed at her, indicating she had more to say. Apparently, resting her case was too much to hope for.

"This is what you always do, Lani. Proclaim that you don't like some guy, which is a big clue that you feel just the opposite."

"That's so far off the mark," she scoffed, even though there was a ring of truth in the words.

"Oh? Then I give you exhibit A—blowing off the Dalton Sunday dinner to meet the Campbell clan. Yeah, Mom told me. Then there's exhibit B—kissing him at the Ace in the Hole. That's all over town. And exhibit C—defending him to Anderson and Travis."

"Wow. Where'd you hear all of this?"

Her sister grinned. "Travis and I are close."

Lani couldn't argue any of that. Her only excuse was working with Russ on the case, but they were keeping the association quiet. She was at a loss to explain why he'd never once brought up brainstorming their strategy during the trip to his family's farm. Or that out-of-the-blue kiss by the stream. But just now when he'd dropped her off she'd been prepared, and he didn't make a move. What was she supposed to think?

Finally, she said, "None of that means anything."

"Right." Lindsay sighed. "Look, sis, I'm only saying this because I'm concerned. Don't make the same mistakes I have."

Lani refilled her glass. "There's nothing between Russ and me, so cheating isn't an issue."

"I meant don't choose an inappropriate man." She held up her hand to stop the words when Lani opened her mouth to argue. "Don't waste your breath. I know the signs, and it's clear you're falling for him. But keep this in mind, Lani. He's an outsider. When his work here in Rust Creek Falls is done, he'll be gone."

Or at least go back to the way it was before—when he'd come into the Ace in the Hole and ignored her.

Lani really wished that this conversation had unfolded in a different way or that her sister hadn't been betrayed one too many times, because having someone to talk to would be helpful. Her feelings for Russ were muddled and confused, and bouncing them off the person she was closest to in the world would really be awesome. But Lindsay was too cynical right now to be objective.

"Okay, then," she said. "It's official. You and I will be charter members of the newly formed Rust Creek Falls Wallflowers Club."

Lindsay grinned and held up her hand. "Pinkie swear?"

"I solemnly vow." Lani hooked fingers and made the promise sacred, binding and official.

They hugged, and her sister said good-night before going upstairs to bed. Lani stayed in the kitchen to finish her wine, mull things over.

And the more she did, the more convinced she was that no way Russ was jealous about her dating Brad Crawford. It was just foolish, wishful thinking on her part. It was also the right move. She'd promised to help Russ find the culprit, and she wouldn't go back on her word. But the sooner this investigation came to a conclusion, the better.

With any luck, that would happen before Detective Dreamy captured her heart completely.

After the school carnival closed down on Saturday night, Russ went to the Ace in the Hole. Alone in the crowd here was better than another evening staring at the walls of his room at Strickland's Boarding House. It wasn't all that different from hanging out at his house in Boulder Junction, but it sure felt lonelier. Somehow, he knew Lani was responsible for the attitude shift but couldn't put his finger on exactly why that was. It didn't matter, really. He just knew that one more night alone with his suspect list and interview notes might drive him nuts.

About a year ago, he'd discovered the bar after working a shift for Gage, and the two of them had come in for a beer. It was a good place to hang out, especially on busy nights like tonight. No one noticed you unless you wanted to be noticed, and if they didn't it was no big deal.

Rosey Traven was behind the bar, talking to one of the other waitresses, Annie Kellerman, who was serving beers and making drinks for customers. And then the hair on the back of his neck stood up and he glanced to his right, where Lani was delivering an order of food at a booth by the window.

Relief slammed through him that she was here and not with Brad Crawford. That was something he needed to talk to her about, but it would have to wait. After setting baskets of burgers and fries in front of the middle-aged couple, she smiled. Although from across the room he couldn't hear her, Russ knew she was telling them to flag her down if they needed anything else.

She glanced around the room, checking her customers,

and spotted him. An instant smile turned up the corners of her mouth, as if she was glad to see him. Then it shut down. Her body language said she wanted to turn her back and head in the other direction, but she must have remembered they had a cover to maintain.

Smiling a big, fat, phony smile, she headed straight for him and threw her arms around his neck. Whispering in his ear she said, "Just to be clear, this is because everyone thinks we're dating."

"Understood."

And he really did. Reading between the lines, that was her letting him know she didn't appreciate his mixed signals. And he wasn't proud of himself for it. That was just what happened when a man was mixed up. Lani messed with his head, scrambled the messages about focusing on his career and the necessity of fighting the longing to have her in his arms.

He put his hands at her waist and smiled. Then he asked the question he would ask if they really were a couple. "When do you get off?"

"Pretty soon."

"Okay. I'll wait for you." He said it loud enough for everyone around them to hear.

Her eyes took on that look they got when she turned stubborn. "You don't have—"

He touched his lips to hers and murmured against her mouth, "It's our cover."

"Right." She smiled and pulled back. "Have a seat at the bar. I'll be as quick as I can."

"Take your time."

She nodded then moved to a table where four women were seated and whipped out her order pad. Russ walked over to the bar and took the empty stool on the end. Annie appeared in front of him. "Hey, Russ. What can I get you? The usual?"

"Yeah."

The usual would be a longneck bottle of beer, and it appeared in front of him. Since he'd started dropping by the bar, more often than not he'd chat with whoever was serving drinks here. Unless that person happened to be Lani. From the first moment he'd seen her, he'd known she was trouble, the kind of woman who could make a fool out of him if he wasn't careful. Now here they were, pretending to be a couple. Fate had a warped sense of humor, because he had the feeling he wasn't pretending anymore.

"Hey, Detective." Rosey Shaw Traven was suddenly in front of him on the other side of the bar. "You look lost in thought."

"Yeah." He hadn't noticed her approach, which wasn't like him. "Got a lot on my mind."

"I imagine you do." She rested her hands on curvy hips, and the movement pulled her peasant blouse down just enough to reveal a hint of ample cleavage. "Any progress on finding out who spiked the punch at the wedding this summer?"

"No."

"You being a hotshot detective and all, that must be frustrating."

In more ways than he'd ever been frustrated before. "You could say that."

"I heard the school carnival has been quiet so far."

"That's right." It closed up a little while ago without incident. But the pressure was still on. "One more day and then we're home free. For now."

"Sunday's traditionally a big day. After church a lot of folks stop by with their families."

"Gage briefed me. We just have to make it until everything shuts down at four tomorrow." He met her gaze. "There's a part of me hoping whoever it is tries something and then we'll have him. Put an end to it." And his time with Lani would end, too. At least under the current rules.

Rosey picked up a tumbler and started to polish the glass with the rag in her hand. "So, I hear you and Lani have been hanging out together."

"You heard right." He took a sip of his beer.

"Why is that?"

"Why's what?" he hedged.

The older woman smiled shrewdly, as if she knew he'd dodged the question deliberately. "It's like this. You come into the Ace for months and never give a pretty girl like Lani a tumble. Then the two of you are stuck in a jail cell for hours while everyone at that wedding reception was three sheets to the wind."

"That can be explained," he protested. Although he still didn't know why she'd taken his keys to the cell.

"No doubt." She put the glass down then picked up another one and started polishing. "But I haven't made my point yet."

"Okay." Whatever it was he knew he wouldn't like it, so the longer it took to get there, the better. "Please continue."

"Thanks. Where was I?" She thought for a moment then nodded. "Right. Locked in a jail cell together. Then two months go by, the sheriff still doesn't know who doctored the punch that day and you haven't shown your face here at the bar. But he hires you to investigate."

"That's true," he agreed.

"Suddenly, you and Lani are hanging out, spending a lot of time together." She met his gaze again. "Why is that, exactly?"

"We're getting to know each other."

"So I heard. Dating." She sounded skeptical, which was actually very perceptive of her.

"Do you have a problem with that?"

"It all depends on how you define *problem*."

"Why don't you tell me how you define it," he suggested.

"I intend to." She put down the glass and the rag then rested her hands on the scarred wood of the bar. "I've known Lani for a few years now. She's a good girl, and I'm very fond of her. I've watched her go out with different men. I've seen her in love or infatuated, even smitten a time or two. Whatever you want to call it when a woman falls for a guy."

Russ didn't like the flare of jealousy that streaked through him at the mention of Lani with other guys. "I'm still waiting for you to get to the point."

There was an odd smile on her face, as if she knew what he was feeling and approved. A moment later it was gone, and all that remained was a warning. "I've seen her in various stages of a relationship, but I've never seen her acting the way she is now with you."

"Maybe that's good."

"Or maybe it isn't." She drilled him with a fiercely protective look. "Lani got her heart stomped on once, and I won't stand by and do nothing while it happens again. *That's* my point."

"Got it."

"So, we're clear?" she demanded.

"Yes, ma'am."

"Good. Nice talking with you. Enjoy your beer." Rosey turned and walked away, hips swaying.

Russ figured that woman had missed her calling and could have had a brilliant career in law enforcement. It wasn't often he knew how it felt to be interrogated, but he did now. And the experience was illuminating but not in the way he would have expected.

First the sheriff had stood up for Lani, and now her boss had made her allegiance clear. Neither of those two could be labeled a fool, which meant that Lani Dalton inspired loyalty in the people around her, not just her family. That would be impossible to pull off if she wasn't trustworthy. So he had to take her off the suspect list even if she was only on it in his head.

But something unexpected happened to him after Rosey's revelation about Lani's love life. Russ knew she'd been dumped—she'd told him when they were in the jail cell that she'd sworn off men. Now, though, he wanted to know more about the jerk who had stomped on her heart.

And he was going to ask when she got off work.

Chapter Ten

It turned out that Lani didn't get off work as soon as she'd expected. The bar got busy, and Rosey asked her to stay. She passed that on to Russ and told him he should leave, but he didn't. That made her feel pretty good before she reminded herself it was dangerous when he was nice to her.

She liked him a lot and desperately wanted to be in his arms again. The thing was, he was attracted to her, too. The kiss at the farm was proof because there hadn't been anyone else around to put on an act for. But he didn't want to want her, and that didn't bode well for anything long-term. An affair didn't interest her. Well, she was *interested*, but giving in to the temptation didn't make it any less stupid an idea.

She grabbed her purse out of the office in the back room, said good-night to her boss then walked out into the main bar area, stopping beside the stool where Russ was sitting.

"I'm heading home." She glanced around the room,

where only a couple of customers remained. "There aren't enough people here to make a difference in maintaining our cover. You really didn't have to stay."

"My alternative was an empty room at the boarding-house."

"Wow, I was the lesser of two evils," she teased, but was secretly touched that he'd admitted being lonely. It tugged at her heart. "Way to make a girl feel special."

"I didn't mean it that way." He stood and put his hand at the small of her back, urging her toward the door. "And you are special."

His voice lowered to a sexy drawl and made her tingle all over. *Don't take it seriously. Danger, Lani Dalton*, she warned herself.

"There you go being nice to me, Detective. That could turn a girl's head."

"Not yours. You're too smart for that."

"Don't bet on it."

Russ opened the door and let her precede him outside. The cool air felt good on her hot cheeks. On nights when it was wall-to-wall people in the bar, it got pretty warm in there. Looking up, she dragged in a breath and let it out slowly. The night sky was clear, and stars sparkled like fairy dust. It was spectacular, and she reminded herself not to take it for granted.

"Montana is really beautiful in September."

"Unpredictable, too. The weather can turn suddenly."

Not just the weather, she thought. A girl never knew what to expect from Detective Campbell. He'd stuck it out and waited for her to get off work when both of them knew this wasn't a relationship. So why had he done that? Was he going to kiss her good-night this time? Should she kiss him? She hoped he would make a move, and so much for trying to stay mad at him for running hot and cold. But she couldn't manage it after he'd admitted being lonely.

Besides, playing games wasn't her style. She just wasn't wired that way.

"My truck is parked around that side of the building," she said, pointing to the right. "I need to get going."

"Before you do, can I ask you a question?"

"About what?"

"The guy who broke your heart."

The chill in the air penetrated her thin sweater, and she shivered. Without a word, Russ slipped off his battered brown leather jacket and dragged it around her shoulders. It felt good, warm from his body. Like being wrapped in his arms. Safe.

"What did Rosey say to you?" She pulled the edges of the jacket closer around her.

He leaned his elbows on the hitching rail in front of the bar. "For one thing, she's suspicious of what's going on with you and me. Your boss is a very observant woman."

"Suspicious how?"

He shrugged. "She noticed me coming in for a while, but you and I didn't get friendly until recently, when Gage hired me to work on the case full-time."

"Is that why you stayed tonight? To prove something to her?"

"Partly." He glanced at her. "But she warned me not to stomp on your heart like the last guy. Now I'm curious about him."

"Rosey is protective of all her girls. Don't worry about her."

"I'm not. But you once told me that a woman doesn't need a man to be happy and fulfilled. That sounds like a disillusioned woman to me."

The subtext was that he was concerned about her, and that sent warm fuzzy feelings sliding through her. "Don't lose any sleep over it."

"That's not why I asked," he said. "But what she told

me is motivation for that remark of yours, and I'd like to know what he did to you."

There was no point in refusing to talk about it. Anyone in town could tell him her sad story.

She leaned back against the hitching rail and met his gaze. "Jason Harvey was a good-looking cowboy who sweet-talked me until hell wouldn't have it. He had me at *darlin'*."

"What happened?"

"He told me he'd come to Rust Creek Falls to buy up land. After the flood two years ago some folks just didn't have it in them to rebuild and walked away from their property. Jase talked a good game about developing it."

"I see."

"I was really interested in him. And as we've already established, I know a lot of people in town. I introduced him to anyone who might be able to get his dream off the ground."

"What happened?"

"Someone who didn't have stars in their eyes asked the sheriff to run a background check on him, and bad stuff turned up. He conned people out of money in a phony real estate scheme. When the heat was on here in town, he disappeared without a word to me." He not only broke her heart, she felt as if he'd damaged her reputation. Some people trusted him because she did. Now she felt stupid, felt as if she'd let her friends down. "Is it weird that his not saying goodbye, not facing me at all, is what bothered me most?"

"Maybe that was simpler and easier for you to grab on to and deal with."

"As opposed to the fact that he made a fool of me, used me," she said.

"Lani, I—" Russ dragged his fingers through his hair. "In a way, I'm using you. I feel guilty about that."

"Completely different. You're not after something and pretending to care about me to get it." She thought about that. "Well, I guess you are, but I'm in on it. By mutual consent we're putting on an act to achieve a common goal. For the greater good."

He didn't look convinced. "Still, I want you to know that your help is appreciated."

"Are you 'breaking up' with me?" she teased. "That sounds an awful lot like things are over. If it would be easier, you could text me."

He flashed a smile and fortunately the moon was bright enough to highlight how adorable he looked. "What kind of guy do you take me for?"

"A good guy." She tapped her lip. "At the very least, we should have a fight. Otherwise how would it look when I go out with Brad Crawford to pump him for information?"

"I thought we agreed you were going to wait on that," he said sharply.

The smile disappeared and she missed it. "We didn't agree on anything. You just said it wasn't a good idea."

"I stand by that." He looked down at her. "And I think you should let that strategy go."

"I disagree. So far, he's the one who seemed to have the most to gain from getting the town drunk. What's the big deal if I talk to him? Butter him up a little to make him let down his guard."

"The big deal is that a date with him could be dangerous if he's guilty and suspects that you're onto him."

"What if I do it in a very public place? The bar, for instance?"

"I still don't like it. You have no experience with this sort of thing, and in my opinion, holding off for now would be best."

"You're the professional," she said, shrugging. "I'll defer

to your judgment. But if we don't get a break soon, I'm going to contact Brad."

"Let's talk it over first."

"Okay. As long as an opportunity doesn't present itself before I can do that."

"Please don't go rogue." His voice was wry.

"I make no promises," she said. "Now I really have to go."

"Okay."

She turned to the right and walked around the building to where her truck sat all by itself. After she unlocked the driver's door with her key fob, Russ opened it for her. This was where one of them usually said something about a plan to meet and compare notes. Right now there was nothing to compare, but she really wanted to know when she would see him again. And his remark about an empty room at the boardinghouse had struck a nerve.

"Would you like to come to Sunday dinner at my house tomorrow?" The words came out before she could think them through and she held her breath, bracing for rejection.

He hesitated. "Are you sure your family would be okay with that?"

She knew he meant Anderson and Travis because Russ hadn't rubbed anyone else the wrong way. "They'll be fine."

He hesitated a moment then said, "I'd like that."

"Good. Come by the house around four."

"I have to wrap up the school carnival, so…"

"Okay. Dinner is around five-thirty."

"Shouldn't be a problem." He leaned down and touched his mouth to hers in a sweet, swift kiss. "Good night."

"'Night." Reluctantly, she handed over his jacket then got in and put the window down. "See you tomorrow."

"I'll be there."

She truly hoped Anderson and Travis didn't hold a

grudge. Otherwise the Dalton family dinner was going to be more exciting than usual.

Lani was nervous. She'd been watching out the front window, waiting for Russ to arrive and be the one to answer the door. It felt as if she'd been waiting forever but the clock only said four-thirty. Technically he wasn't late, but she was still anxious.

Finally, the familiar truck pulled up out front, and her heart started pounding. She brushed her sweaty palms down the sides of her jeans and hurried into the family room. Travis and Anderson were sitting on the couch, watching a football game.

Leaning on the back of the sofa she said, "Russ is here. Remember what I said. Be nice to him. He was only doing his job."

Travis gave her an irritated glare. "We get it. Geez, Lani. We're not idiots."

Anderson grinned. "Don't worry, sis. We'll be good. Do you want to talk about why our behavior is so important to you?"

No, she thought, it was the last thing she wanted to discuss. Before she could say that, the doorbell rang.

"I'll get it." She shrugged at them then hurried down the hall.

After stopping in front of the door, she released a deep, cleansing breath before opening it. Russ stood there in all his masculine splendor: jeans, boots and leather jacket. The word *handsome* didn't do him justice, and the whole package made her girl parts quiver with excitement.

"Hi," she said in a voice that was hardly more than a whisper.

"Hey. Hope I'm not late. The carnival breakdown took longer than I figured."

"Everything okay?" That was when she realized a part

of her was holding a breath, uneasy about the possibility of another incident.

"Fine." He came inside. "Quiet."

"Well, brace yourself. That's about to change." She angled her head toward the kitchen-family room, which was the heart of this home—and where everyone was waiting for them. "On the upside, you only have to meet four of my siblings. My sister Lindsay is away, at law school."

"Walking in her father's footsteps?" he said.

"Yes." Obviously, he'd remembered her telling him that she wouldn't be in jail long because her father was an attorney and would get her out. Not something she wanted to discuss further right now. "Are you ready for this?" she asked.

"I'm a cop. Ready for anything."

"It's a good motto. Let's see if it holds up." Lani led the way down the hall and stopped in the doorway. "Everyone, this is Russ Campbell." The announcement was followed by a chorus of greetings from the group. "Some of you already know him—Travis and Anderson—and we'll make the rounds for the rest of you."

They started with her parents, who were in the kitchen working together on preparing dinner. "Russ, this is my dad, Ben, and my mom, Mary."

"Nice to meet you, Russ." Her father shook his hand.

"We're glad you could join us for dinner," her mother said. "Lani says you have a big family."

"Yes, ma'am. Two brothers and a sister. But you and Mr. Dalton have my parents beat."

Ben glanced at everyone in the family room. "Wouldn't trade any one of them."

"Maybe Travis," Lani teased.

"He would say the same about his annoying little sister," her mother pointed out.

"True," she admitted. "And I take great pride in whatever I can do to make him feel that way."

"I have to get these potatoes mashed," Mary said. "Please excuse me."

"Can I help, Mom?"

"Not this time, sweetie. You make introductions and when you're finished, dinner will probably be ready."

"Okay. Follow me," she said to Russ. In the family room she stopped by the large corner group in front of the TV. "You know Travis and Anderson."

Both men stood and politely shook hands.

"Nice to see you again." Travis smiled, and it didn't look forced.

"Same here." In spite of the casual words, Russ looked wary. He held out his hand to Anderson. "How's it going?"

"Good. You? Any progress on the investigation?"

"No, but I wish. Rust Creek Falls really needs closure on what happened. Everyone is paranoid."

"And that's not how the people of this town are used to feeling," Anderson commented. "About the last time we talked… We might have given you the wrong impression. The thing is, everyone is grateful for your focus on this."

"I second that," Travis said. "You just kind of caught the two of us off guard, and we got a little defensive. Didn't mean anything by it."

"I appreciate that."

Russ seemed to relax, and Lani wanted to give both of her brothers a big hug. They gave her a hard time, but that was their job as her siblings. They would do anything for her, and she felt the same about them.

She sent each of them an appreciative look. "Sorry to interrupt the game."

"You should be." But Anderson's grin telegraphed his teasing.

She took Russ's hand, and they walked over to a corner

of the family room where her mom kept a toy box for her one-year-old grandson. Her sister and brother-in-law were sitting on the carpet, supervising the little guy.

"This is my sister Paige, her handsome husband, Sutter, and their adorable baby, Carter Benjamin."

The little boy had fairly recently started walking, and at the sound of his name he looked way up at the stranger then promptly fell on his tush.

"Hey, buddy." Russ went down on one knee and held out a hand to the child. "You okay?"

"He's used to it, poor baby. I take comfort from the fact that he won't remember." Paige was a sixth-grade teacher at Rust Creek Falls Elementary School. She was looking at Russ. "I've heard a lot about you."

"Don't believe everything—unless it's good."

When he smiled, Lani swore the world stopped turning on its axis, or maybe her heart spinning out of control just made it feel that way.

"I hear you've got a tough job." Sutter had light brown hair and blue eyes. He made his living training horses.

Russ shrugged noncommittally. "Just wish there was progress to report." He smiled when the baby slapped a tiny hand in his big palm. "High five, pal. Or should I say low five?"

The baby grinned and did it again.

"He's got teeth," Lani said to her sister, admiring her nephew's two on top and a matching set on the bottom.

"Funny how that happens on his way to eating solid food," her sister responded wryly.

Lani leaned down and brushed baby-fine strands of hair off his forehead. "He's growing up too fast. Please tell me you're not going to cut his hair."

"Ever?" Sutter and Russ said together in matching tones of male disapproval.

"Well-done, sis," Paige said, supporting the effort to get a rise out of the two men.

"It was too easy."

Carter had used Russ's hand to pull himself to a standing position then grunted and indicated he wanted to be picked up. That was unusual, since the kid was normally shy with strangers. But Russ obliged, proving that he'd been telling the truth when he claimed to be ready for anything.

The baby touched his nose, made a funny face after brushing his small palm over the slight stubble on Russ's jaw then studied his hand while flexing his fingers. The big man patiently waited while the little guy scratched the leather collar of his jacket and slapped at his shoulder. He seemed to know when Carter was bored and gently set him on his feet, protectively holding him until he was steady.

"You're good with kids," Paige observed.

Lani's heart melted a little more. "You're a man of many unexpected talents."

"Kids are easy," he answered. "It's adults who get complicated."

She couldn't argue with that. "I'm still on introduction detail. Where are Caleb and Mallory?"

"They took Lily outside. She's playing soccer this year and wanted to practice her ball skills," Paige explained.

"Okay." She looked at Russ. "This is the last one, I promise. But again I say brace yourself. Lily is really something. Very precocious. There's just no way to prepare for her."

He didn't look the least bit intimidated, which was impressive. "Lead on."

They walked out the French door leading to the backyard and a brick-lined patio. There was an expanse of grass and a gazebo in the far corner of the enclosed area. Her brother Caleb, his wife, Mallory, and their nine-year-old daughter, Lily, were standing on the grass, kicking the black-and-white ball back and forth.

"Hi, Aunt Lani," the little girl said. "Grandma told us your boyfriend was coming over. Is that him?"

"This is Russ." She wasn't quite sure how to address the *boyfriend* comment.

"I'm Mallory," her auburn-haired sister-in-law said. "And this is our daughter, Lily. Sweetie, your grandma said that Aunt Lani's *friend* was going to be here."

The adorable black-haired, almond-eyed child had been adopted by Mallory's sister and her husband. After they died in a car accident, her aunt took on guardianship. She and Caleb had finalized the adoption after they were married.

The little girl lived up to her billing as precocious. "He's her friend and he's a boy. Doesn't that make him her boyfriend?"

That was a literal assessment, and Lani was trying to figure out how to address the personal nuances of what her niece had said.

Her brother, bless him, stuck out his hand and said, "I'm Caleb."

"Nice to meet you."

"You're a policeman," Lily commented.

"Yes. A detective."

"Do you arrest bad people?" she wanted to know.

"If they're caught breaking the law."

"Do you put them in jail?"

Russ looked at her, and the expression in his eyes said he was thinking about that night they'd spent together in the cell. Lani didn't think she was a bad person, but what she'd done was filed under wrong thing, right reason.

Russ met the little girl's gaze. "Sometimes."

"How come not all the time?" the little interrogator wanted to know.

"Okay, Lily," her mother said. "You're going to make Russ's ears tired."

The child looked up with a puzzled expression on her pretty face. "Ears don't get tired."

"Trust me," Mal said, "they do."

Lily shrugged. "I'm going inside to see baby Carter."

"And I'm going to see if your grandmother needs any help getting dinner on the table," her mother said.

Caleb picked up the ball. "Nice to meet you, Russ. I hope my daughter's questions didn't bother you."

"Not at all," he said. "But it wouldn't surprise me to see her become an investigator someday."

Her brother grinned. "No kidding."

The rest of the evening went just as smoothly as the introductions. Russ got along with everyone, including the children. He seemed to fit in really well, and Lani realized a part of her wished he hadn't. She'd been anticipating a reason to cross him off as incompatible with her family, which would definitely be a relationship deal breaker.

She was looking for a flaw in him because her feelings were growing deeper, but she had no clue how he really felt. He gave her a kiss here, a compliment there. Saying she was special. What did that mean? And why did he refuse to open up about himself?

But she knew one thing for sure. Until the spiked punch mystery was solved, she wouldn't know whether he was just seeing her because of the investigation. If so, he would disappear when it was over, and she needed to know one way or the other.

It was time to speed things up on the case. That meant chatting up Brad Crawford even if Russ didn't like the idea.

Chapter Eleven

When opportunity taps you on the shoulder, you don't just walk away. Not when it was important to Russ's investigation. The day after Lani decided it was time to go for broke and talk to Brad Crawford opportunity presented itself and she wasn't going to miss it.

Oddly enough, her chance came on Monday, traditionally the least busy day of the week at the Ace in the Hole. She'd just finished her shift when the guy in question came in. Of all the gin joints in all the world, Brad had to walk into hers, right? Except gin joints in Rust Creek Falls were limited.

She said hello to him because they had a passing acquaintance, and he said hello back. It was now or never, so she asked him if he'd like to have a beer with her. When she said she was buying, he agreed.

After texting Russ to let him know about this lucky break and a vow to fill him in later about what she learned, she grabbed a couple of longnecks and joined Brad in a quiet corner booth. Her cell phone buzzed before she could sit down across from him, but she ignored it.

She held up her bottle. "What should we drink to?"

"Why do we have to drink to anything?"

"We don't," she said.

Hopefully, that wasn't a sign that he was going to be difficult. Brad was about as tall as Russ and too handsome for his own good. He had brown hair, green eyes and was really built, as in broad shoulders, wide chest and muscular legs inside those worn jeans.

He was six years older than Lani and she hadn't gone to school with him but had heard talk. And like every unattached woman in town, she was aware of his story and his reputation. He'd been über popular in high school and had never been without a girlfriend. It was common knowledge that he was in no hurry to settle down, so it had been a big surprise when he married Janie Delane seven years ago.

They divorced three years later because, rumor had it, she was fed up with him only wanting someone to cook, clean and do laundry. Apparently, she'd told him he should have just hired a housekeeper. That would have been cheaper and easier for both of them.

"I was just trying to start a conversation," Lani said. Her cell phone buzzed again, and she ignored it again. "How've you been?"

"Since when?" He leaned back in the booth and sipped his beer.

"I don't know. How about today?"

"I'm fine."

"Anything new with you?" she asked.

"Like what?"

Wow, he was being difficult. "Are you seeing anyone? Is there anyone special in your life?"

"Are you offering?" His smile was charming but didn't

hide the slightest bit of wariness in his eyes. "I heard you and that Kalispell detective hooked up."

Though in the current colloquial definition of that phrase, Brad heard right, she didn't consider the two of them a romantic item. But since they'd been acting that way for the sake of this investigation, the rumor needed to be addressed for purposes of this conversation.

"Russ and I are friends. Kind of." She thought for a moment. "We're just having fun."

"Let's drink to that." Brad held up his beer bottle. "To having fun. Nothing complicated. And no demands."

"To that." Lani touched the neck of her bottle to his and tried to be enthusiastic, but wasn't sure she pulled it off. He was one cynical son of a gun. If she had to guess, the edge of bitterness he conveyed probably had something to do with his divorce. Then she realized he'd bobbed and weaved and avoided answering her question.

"How about you?" she asked. "Hooked up with anyone?"

"Hooked up? Yeah." He toyed with the bottle on the table between them. "Serious about? No way."

"You sound determined about that."

"Because I am. Like I said—all fun, all the time. No strings. No drama."

Lani didn't know if that was a warning or an invitation. She wasn't the least bit interested, though. Even if she was attracted to his charm and good looks, that lone-wolf-Lothario thing he had going on was a total turnoff. Although it occurred to her that Russ was something of a loner, too, and that man turned her on just by walking in the door. Go figure.

She didn't have to be attracted to Brad to get information out of him and would play any game he wanted in order to do just that.

"Okay, so personally you're not tied down and have no

intentions of ever committing. But professionally it seems you're doing all right."

"Oh?" His green eyes narrowed on her.

"Yeah. I heard about that poker game on the Fourth of July. The word is that you did pretty well."

"You mean because I took Old Man Sullivan's ranch." It wasn't a question.

"That's what I mean," she said, trying to assess his emotions. Angry? Guilty? Ashamed? She couldn't decide.

"Have you ever played cards, Lani? I mean for real money?"

"No," she admitted.

"That's what I thought." He took a long swallow of beer. "Rule number one—never wager anything you can't afford to lose."

"Even so…it's the man's home," Lani pointed out.

He met her gaze squarely. "I can't help it if I'm a more skilled player. I couldn't swear to it, but it's as if the old man wanted to lose."

"Too bad we can't ask him. He's disappeared," she said. "No one has heard from him for a while."

Brad shrugged. Lani wasn't sure what she'd expected, although a written confession from Brad that he'd slipped a mickey to the whole town so that he could win at poker would have been awfully tidy. Most people would have been ambivalent about winning and taking a man's property. But this guy didn't show any sign of letting his conscience get in the way of raking in his poker winnings.

She'd never actually believed he was the perpetrator. After all, despite the feud between the Crawfords and the Traubs that was so old, no one could clearly remember how it started, he was part of a nice family. They were upstanding citizens and, as far as she knew, had never been in trouble with the law.

But every barrel had a bad apple, and it could be that

she was looking right at him, Lani thought. Maybe it was time to mention how everyone got drunk that night and gauge his reaction.

"Isn't it crazy what happened after the wedding? How so many people you'd never expect got drunk and began behaving out of character?" Including herself, she thought, hoping he wouldn't point that out.

"Wasn't your boyfriend hired to find out who spiked that punch?" It was hard to tell whether his tone leaned more toward suspicion or curiosity.

"The sheriff thought his skill as a detective would come in handy, since his own investigation wasn't getting anywhere. People are squirrelly. Worried that there could be a repeat of what happened. Or even worse. Did you have any of the punch?"

"Yeah."

She wanted to ask if he'd had enough to get drunk but didn't want to come off as an interrogator even though she was. "Doesn't it creep you out that someone put something in that punch and most of the town ended up acting weird? What if someone had gotten hurt because of it?"

"It's...unsettling," he allowed.

"Not to mention a crime," she said.

"After all this time and from what I hear not a single clue, does your boyfriend really think he can find out who did it?"

Was there a deliberate challenge in those words? Could it be he was toying with her because he was responsible for getting everyone drunk? Or just messing with her because he was mad at the world? Now was the time to ask.

As she was formulating the question, some part of her mind registered the fact that the bar's screen door had just opened and closed, admitting a customer even though it was getting pretty late.

"I wouldn't call Russ my boyfriend," Lani started. "We're just—"

At that exact moment Detective Russ Campbell walked up to the booth and leaned down for a quick kiss. "Hi, babe. Got here as quick as I could."

Lani slid over to make room because he was obviously planning to sit down beside her. It took her a few moments to form a coherent response because her brain was short-circuited from the sizzle of that unexpected kiss.

"You made good time."

"Helps when you're the law." Brad eyed the newcomer skeptically.

"I don't think we've met. Russ Campbell," he said, holding his hand out across the table.

The other man shook it. "Brad Crawford. Nice to meet you, Detective."

Russ stared at him, and even though she could only see his profile, Lani noticed tension in his jaw and felt the hostility. Then he looked at her and she also felt the heat of his irritation and disapproval. "So, what were you two talking about?"

"Oh, you know," she said. "This and that. It was no big deal."

"Yeah," Brad agreed. "Small talk. Like who spiked the punch after the wedding."

"Did you come up with any suspects?" Russ asked, his eyes narrowing on her.

"No. I guess Brad and I still can't believe that someone who is our friend and possibly a neighbor would do something like that." She looked at the man sitting across from them.

"I was just telling Lani that it seems unlikely you'll find the perp, since so much time has gone by."

"Not if that person slips up and tries it again," Russ said. "We're ready for that."

"Okay, then." Brad pressed his lips together and nodded. "I've got to get going. A lot to do tomorrow on the ranch."

"And the land you won in the poker game gives you even more responsibility," Lani said.

"Yeah." Brad slid out of the booth and looked at each of them. "Thanks for the beer, Lani. See you around, Detective."

Then he walked straight to that noisy, rusty Ace in the Hole screen door, opened it and headed out into the night. Lani and Russ sat side by side, alone and still no closer to finding out who had gotten the whole town drunk.

It was several moments before Russ said anything and when he did, she wished he hadn't.

"What the hell were you thinking, Lani?"

"I was thinking a lot of things. You might want to be more specific."

"Confronting Brad Crawford by yourself. Is that specific enough for you?" he demanded.

She shifted on the booth seat, and her shoulder brushed against his. It wasn't clear if the sparks she felt were her attraction or his irritation. If she'd been straight across from him, she would have made a point of direct eye contact, so she was pretty glad they were side by side. That way she didn't have to see the expression on his face confirming that he couldn't stand the sight of her.

"I was thinking that the investigation was stalled, and Brad Crawford won a ranch in a poker game. That's strong motive." She glanced at his profile and saw the muscle jerk in his jaw. "And you forgot to say thank you."

"What the hell for? Putting yourself in a potentially dangerous situation?" He didn't sound angry as much as concerned for her safety. "You promised to talk to me first."

"Brad came in just as I was getting off work, and I took that as a sign."

"Of what? That you should play detective?" He gave

her a sideways look. "There are any number of ways that a solo interrogation could have gone south if he's the guy we're looking for."

"This is a public place. I thought about that."

"Public but practically empty." He glanced around. "Whoever is tending bar went in the back for something. That would give a suspect the perfect opportunity to overpower you."

"I'd scream for help. It's not like this place is a deserted alley," she scoffed.

"What if he had a weapon and told you not to make a sound?"

"Oh." She hadn't thought about that.

"Yeah. Oh."

"But he didn't do anything," she pointed out. "I'm fine."

"Because I got here in time to stop you from—"

She waited but he didn't finish the statement. "To stop me from what?"

"Never mind."

Now it was her turn to be irritated. The way he shut down like that was really starting to bug her. If he wanted a fight, she'd be happy to oblige and maybe clear the air. But he wouldn't fight fair. Or at all. "If there's nothing else, I'd like to go home now."

She waited for him to slide out of the booth and let her leave, but he didn't budge. And he was too big for her to push him out of her way.

"Please move so I can get out of here."

"Tell me what Brad said."

"You're welcome." His grunt made her smile. "He said a lot of things and for the record, he seems like kind of an arrogant jerk. I asked him how he could take away someone's land and home and he said Sullivan was asking for it."

"How?"

"By wagering something he couldn't afford to lose and

not being a very good poker player." She shrugged. "That sounds a lot like motive to me."

"As much as I don't like that guy, and make no mistake—" he looked at her sideways "—I don't like him a lot, there are a couple of holes in your theory."

"What?"

He rubbed his chin thoughtfully. "That was a pickup poker game, meaning there was nothing arranged ahead of time. If Brad did spike the punch, it would only have given him an advantage in that the other guys would be drunk and sloppy players. He couldn't know who those players would be or how much they would bet on a hand."

"I see what you mean. Still," she said, "that reasoning doesn't let him off the hook, either."

"How so?"

"He seemed edgy to me. Sort of cynical and bitter. He might have a grudge against someone."

"Do you know anything about his personal life?" Speaking of edgy, Russ's voice had a tinge of tension. "Is he dating anyone?"

"He dates everyone. In fact, he wanted to drink to having fun with no strings attached." She was remembering his exact words. "I asked if he was seeing anyone special and he asked if I was offering."

"Son of a—" Russ's fingers curled into a fist.

"Don't go all macho." The words came out of her mouth but inside she was cheering his tense reaction. It meant something. She was almost sure of it. "I was the one who offered to buy him a beer."

"Don't remind me." He looked thoughtful. "You said he's divorced? Could be he wants to get even with someone for that."

"I got the impression that he's just lonely. And doesn't even know it."

"Interesting assessment when he's playing the field. Lonely in a crowd?" he asked wryly.

"Sure. Quantity doesn't make up for quality. Guys won't admit that publicly. It's a very closely guarded manly secret."

"What is?"

"That men want to settle down. Have someone special to share their life with."

Come to think of it, men weren't the only ones who felt that way. Lani was lonely. If she admitted that out loud, Russ would laugh, especially after having dinner with a crowd of Daltons.

She was grateful for her family and knew they'd be there for her always. But it was different from having a guy there when she woke up in the morning and someone to come home to at night. With Jase she'd had a glimpse of what making a home together might have looked like, which is why there was such a big hole in her life when he left. Since then she'd never let anyone become that important. Then Russ came along and scooped her out of the fountain.

"If it's a manly secret, how do you know about it?" Russ asked.

"I have brothers. There's talk. Sometimes they don't know I'm listening."

"Last time I checked, that was known as eavesdropping."

There was a teasing tone in his voice and even from the side she could see his mouth curve up in a smile. And even from this vantage point the adorable factor in that smile was plenty powerful.

"I like to think of it more as research into the male point of view. This may come as a shock to you, Detective, but guys are not easy to understand."

He laughed out loud, and the sound was magic to her heart. How she wished to hear him like this more often.

"Compared to women," he said, "understanding guys is as easy as falling off a log."

"So why was he on that log in the first place?" she mused. "Did he get pushed off or jump? And how did the log feel about a two-hundred-pound guy standing there?"

"I rest my case. When a woman plays the feelings card, there goes all rational thought."

"So you're a just-the-facts-ma'am kind of guy?"

"I'm a detective. You can't make a case against the bad guys based on feelings and supposition."

And that brought her down to earth with a gigantic thud. For just a few minutes she'd been able to pretend that they were just any guy and girl sitting in a bar and flirting. But that was an illusion. He was a detective hired to solve the town mystery and was only giving her the time of day because she had a job that gave her unique access to the general public. And tonight she was pretty sure she'd eliminated one of the prime suspects.

Her work there was done.

"Speaking of making cases, it seems there's not one to be made against Brad Crawford. At least not from what he and I talked about tonight."

"And speaking of that, there's something I've been wondering about."

"Oh?" She must have left out a detail in her recounting of the conversation with the poker-playing cowboy.

"When I walked up a little while ago you were denying that I was your boyfriend. You were just about to define what we are."

"Thanks to your timely arrival I didn't have to. So I guess you saved me tonight, after all." Her boyfriend. If only. Getting a glimpse of something she couldn't have was a real mood breaker, and she was ready to be gone. "And now, if you'll excuse me, you have my report. I need to go."

Again he didn't budge. "What would you have told Brad about us? What are we, Lani?"

"I don't know. Co-investigators?" She shrugged. "I told him we were getting to know each other. Just friends." Chancing a look at him, she asked, "Are we?"

"That's not quite right."

Exasperating man. What did that mean? She thought about what he'd started to say earlier. That he'd come here to stop her from doing…something. He hadn't finished the sentence, and now she wanted to know what he'd been about to say.

"Why did you really come here tonight, Russ? We both know I wasn't in any danger from Brad. He's not an idiot or a psychopath. Even if he's guilty there's no way he would have hurt me, especially here. What did you come here to stop me from doing?"

He looked at her, and his hazel eyes glittered, making them more green than brown. Intensity rolled off him so thick she could almost touch it.

"I was going to stop you from leaving with Brad," he finally said.

"I wouldn't have done that," she protested. "Sure, I bought him a beer, but that didn't mean anything. I could have told him there was no spark. You didn't have to bother coming over."

"Yeah, I did."

"Why? I had him right where I wanted him."

"I came because there's somewhere I want you, Lani. And it isn't here at the Ace in the Hole."

The truth was beginning to dawn on her. "Are you jealous of Brad?"

"Yes." The single word was almost a hiss.

"There's no reason to be. Telling him there's no spark would have been the honest-to-God truth. I wouldn't go anywhere with him—"

His finger on her lips stopped the words. “Will you go with me?”

“Where?” she whispered.

“My room. My bed.” Just like that, there was more brown in his eyes than green, highlighting the heat, want and need he couldn’t hide. “Say yes, Lani.”

All she could do was nod.

Chapter Twelve

His room and his bed were temporarily located at Strickland's Boarding House.

Lani would love to see his house in Boulder Junction, but was really glad they didn't have to go that far right now. The drive from the bar didn't take long, and soon they made it to his room on the second floor. As far as they knew, no one had seen them. Not that it would be a problem, since word was all over town that they were a couple. But Melba Strickland had standards at her boardinghouse that didn't include tolerance for a man and woman cozying up too intimately before taking marriage vows.

Russ closed the door behind him and blew out a breath. "We made it."

Lani laughed quietly. "Is Melba in the habit of patrolling the halls?"

"I wouldn't put it past her," he said. "In the morning at breakfast she looks everyone over, and I swear she knows who broke the rules."

"That's just your imagination. There's no way she could tell just by looking."

"I'm not so sure. After a once-over, she has this subtle way of letting us know that what happens in the marriage bed is sacred."

Lani grinned. "If that woman isn't eighty years old, she's darn close. And her husband, Gene, thinks a woman's place is in the home raising babies. Times have changed."

"But those two haven't," he swore. "And let's just say I'd rather be involved in a high-speed car chase than face Melba in the hall while you're in my room."

She looked around. "And a lovely room it is."

The bedside lamp illuminated the comfortable interior including a bed with brass head- and footboards. It was big and covered by a wedding-ring quilt. There was an oak armoire and matching dresser with a ceramic pitcher and washbasin on top. One modern touch was the flat-screen TV mounted on the wall across from the bed.

"This is nice. Homey," she said. "An improvement from the jail cell."

All these weeks he'd pretended nothing had happened that night, forcing her to pretend, too. Now here they were, and she had Brad Crawford to thank for it. She had a feeling if Russ hadn't seen them talking, he wouldn't have brought her here. Seeing her with another man had flipped a switch in him, and she was finally where she wanted to be.

He carefully removed the decorative throw pillows from the bed and set them on the ottoman that matched the red, floral-print chair in the corner.

When he was finished, he stood in front of her at the foot of the bed. "I'm going to make that up to you."

"What?"

"The jail."

"Ah." She shrugged. "There's nothing to make up for. That was pretty awesome."

"You'll get no argument from me, but the ambience left something to be desired." He cupped her face in his big hands. "This time it's private."

She knew what he meant. No danger of anyone walking in on them. That night when they were locked up together and Russ kissed her, all she could think about was being with him. There was no space in her passion-filled mind to think about the fact that they were in a public place.

That time she'd been wearing a sundress, but now she had on a blouse and jeans. Since there was no fear of discovery and they could take their time…

She started unbuttoning her cotton shirt and was working on the last one before glancing up at Russ. He was holding his breath, anticipation stamped on his features. The intensity of his gaze made her knees go all wobbly.

He leaned down and lightly kissed the spot where her neck and shoulder met. "You're killing me here."

"I can speed this up if—"

He touched his tongue to her earlobe then softly blew on it. "I know it didn't sound that way, but I wasn't complaining."

"So I'm getting mixed messages here. Are you in a hurry, or—"

"I'm just so damn glad to be here with you. So damn glad you didn't leave with Brad." He met her gaze, and there was fire in his. He pulled her close and buried his face in her hair. "I've thought about you this way so many times, and it's been driving me crazy. You smell like flowers and sunshine. Just the way you did before. I tried to forget, to get you out of my mind, but you just wouldn't stay put."

So she hadn't been the only one affected by what happened that night. It hadn't been just a fluke, a fling, a one-night thing. Her heart swelled at his words and beat even harder than it already was.

"And would you like to know what I've thought about the most?" he asked.

"What?" The single word was hardly louder than the sound of a sigh.

"Undressing you and taking my time."

"Oh, my."

"Any objections?" One corner of his mouth curved up.

"No."

His smile was completely adorable as he brushed her hands away and undid the last button on her shirt. Then he slid it off her shoulders and unhooked her bra. He dropped it on the floor and stared at her as if he couldn't look hard enough. "Beautiful," he breathed.

As he released the button at the waist of her jeans, she toed off her sneakers and kicked them away so he could take off the rest of her clothes. His gaze slowly moved over her, and there was no mistaking the approval in his eyes.

"Wow," he said.

The removal of his clothes went a lot quicker, and before you could say boo there they were, neither of them wearing a stitch. She had to admit slow and deliberate had its advantages over doing the deed behind bars. This time she could really look at him, the wide shoulders and contour of his chest with its dusting of hair. She'd read magazine articles with pictures of actors and models with a six-pack, but had never seen one up close and personal before. The temptation to touch was simply too strong to resist.

She put her palms on his chest, letting the hair tickle her fingers before sliding down to his taut abdomen. "Very impressive, Detective Campbell."

"Glad you think so, Miss Dalton." When she traced a finger down his side to his waist, he sucked in a breath. "Now you're playing with fire."

"Am I?"

"Yes. But two can play that game," he said.

He cupped her breasts in his palms and lightly rubbed the tips with his thumbs. The touch sent shock waves vibrating through her. For the first time she knew what "putty in his hands" actually meant. Her body felt boneless, as if she could collapse in a puddle at his feet.

Just the excuse she needed. "We're wasting that perfectly good bed."

Without another word she grabbed his hand, walked to the side of it and climbed in then moved over to make room. The mattress dipped from his weight, and just before he pulled her into his arms, she had the fleeting thought that the sheets were cold. Then he slid his arms around her and drew her close to him, and all she could think about was heat.

When he touched his lips to hers she couldn't think at all. The man was nothing if not a good kisser. That was probably the reason she hadn't been able to resist him the first time. But now she knew him better and had the privacy to really appreciate that the man knew what he was doing.

He took his time, leisurely kissing her lips, cheek, jaw and neck. She was already having trouble catching her breath when he took her mouth again, and there was nothing leisurely about it.

He traced her lips with his tongue then dipped inside when she opened to him. At the same time he brushed his hand down her side and over her hip. Her flesh was sensitized and seemed to catch fire everywhere he touched.

While he was kissing the living daylights out of her, Lani let her fingers roam over his shoulders and arms. The muscles and sheer masculinity delighted and amazed her. He was so strong yet deliciously gentle. Feelings that she'd been so careful to hold back seemed to spill over, like lava from a volcano. It was beautiful and dangerous.

He seemed to feel the shift in her mood, and his kisses grew more intense. The sound of their ragged breathing filled the room, and touching became more frantic. He nudged her to her back, and she rested her hands at his waist, urging him toward her. After settling between her legs, he entered her.

At first his movements were slow, as they got used to the feel of each other. Then he picked up the pace and intensity. Lani's body moved easily with his, remembering the rhythm from that night when it was hot outside and he'd unexpectedly kissed her. She couldn't hold back now any more than she could then.

Breathing became a definite challenge. He thrust harder, driving her higher, until finally pleasure exploded through her and rocked her world. She cried out and he kissed her, absorbing all the sounds of her overwhelming reaction that she couldn't hold back.

And then he started to move inside her again. She clutched his hips and met him thrust for thrust. Seconds later he groaned, and she wrapped her arms around his shoulders, and her legs circled his waist. He held her tight until the shudders of satisfaction stopped rolling through him.

It was late when Russ watched Lani roll out of bed. This was the first time since he'd started his official investigation that this warm country-themed room hadn't felt lonely and empty.

He couldn't help admiring her shapely backside even as he wanted to pull her back into his arms and make love to her again. All that soft skin and those feminine curves were really something.

But she had to be at the ranch early, and he had to take

her back to the Ace in the Hole, where her truck was still parked. So they dressed quickly then stood a whisper apart at the foot of the bed with the tangled sheets just inches away.

They smiled at each other as satisfaction hummed between them. Her shiny brown hair was tousled and sexy, just the way it should be after fantastic sex. He reached out and touched a finger to her bottom lip, slightly swollen from his kisses. Her cheeks were pink and her eyes sparkled—in other words, she looked beautiful.

It was time to admit the truth to himself—he had feelings for Lani Dalton. If that wasn't the case, no way would he have given in to temptation again. First being that night in jail.

The problem was that she had secrets. Not knowing what they were made it impossible to trust her, so getting more deeply involved was a bad idea.

"You're awfully quiet," she said. "Do you hate yourself?"

Not quite, but he was in unfamiliar territory here. "Is there some reason I should?"

"Isn't that what people say when they try to resist doing what we just did? That you'll hate yourself in the morning?"

"Right." Russ got it now. "No, I don't hate myself. Do you?"

"It's after midnight, so technically morning has arrived, but I don't hate myself." She smiled and linked her fingers with his. "I just wish I didn't have to go."

"So don't. Stay." He was a little surprised at how much he meant that. A fiercely intense longing tightened in his chest.

"I can't. We might not hate ourselves now, but if we get caught in your room, Melba Strickland could change that. Besides, I have to get my truck."

"I'll take you. Later." He couldn't help feeling they only had now, and he wanted to put off saying good-night.

"You'll get more sleep if we do this now. There's no point in both of us being exhausted."

She was right, but he didn't care about sleep. And that wasn't good. It was time to find out what she was hiding before he got in any deeper than he already was. Maybe she felt the same way about him. She'd been curious about why he left the police force in Denver. He wanted to tell her about it, get that weight off his shoulders. Let her know that keeping secrets inside made them more powerful than they had any right to be. Quid pro quo.

He would tell his story, then she could share hers. "There's something I want to talk to you about."

"Okay."

And that was one of the things he found so irresistible about her. It was late. She had to be tired after working at the ranch then a couple hours at the bar. And she had to be at work again at dawn and was already facing the prospect of very little sleep. But he wanted to say something, and she agreed without question or hesitation.

He took her hand and led her over to the floral-patterned chair in the corner, sitting her in it after he moved the throw pillows to the bed. He lowered himself to the ottoman in front of her and leaned forward, elbows on his knees.

"About why I left the Denver PD..."

When several moments went by she said, "You don't have to tell me. You know that, right?"

"Yes. But I want you to know." Because when you felt a pull as strong as he did for Lani, she had a right to his past. And he had a right to hers. "I found out my partner was on the take."

Her eyes grew wide. "What?"

"He was being paid for information about undercover drug operations, raids, imminent arrests, evidence for trial and even perjuring himself in court."

"How did you find out?" she asked.

"Little things at first. He wasn't where he said he was going to be. A big new house that seemed too much for a cop's salary. Expensive car. Bits of phone conversations. I got suspicious, followed him. Got pics of him meeting with a known drug dealer and cash changing hands."

"Oh, Russ. What happened?" She reached out and linked her fingers with his.

"I went to the watch commander with what I had."

Lani's clear brown eyes were full of sympathy and concern. "What did he say? Something bad happened or you wouldn't have left Denver."

"I guess you don't have to be a detective to figure that out." He smiled but knew it was grim. "He told me to leave it to him."

"And?"

"When nothing happened I tried again. He said I should just stay out of it. My job was to uphold the law so I went over his head to Internal Affairs. But they could never make a case against him. He got careful and no evidence was found. And that's when it all went to hell."

"I don't understand," she said. "You did the right thing. How could that be bad?"

"Cops have a code. You watch each other's back. No matter what." He blew out a breath. "I broke the code. Ratted him out."

"He was a bad cop, breaking the law." She was adamant, on his side. "He's the one who did wrong."

"But all of them had been together for years. I was the newcomer. An upstart. Going for the big score, a promotion at the expense of a brother. I was downgraded in rank and took a pay cut. A subtle way of trying to force me out, but I refused to go. So the precinct cops circled the wagons. They closed ranks, refused to partner with me and, if forced to, slanted incident reports to make me look dirty."

"Oh, my God. That's awful, Russ."

"The thing is most of those guys are good cops. But the mind-set of supporting a brother in arms is more sacred than finding out the truth. In the beginning I backed them up in tough spots and they did the same for me. I thought I'd built up trust, made friends, but it turned out the truth wasn't the most important thing to them."

"But it is to you." She nodded. "It must have been hard being shut out like that. I can't even imagine."

"I could deal with that. But the situation became dangerous. Damned if I did, damned if I didn't. The trust was gone on both sides, which put people at risk. No one had faith in me to watch their back and based on what happened, I didn't believe they had mine. I responded to a domestic violence situation, and a woman and child were endangered because I was alone. No backup. And you never know what you're walking into. I was lucky on that one. It resolved safely."

"So you resigned," she guessed.

He nodded. "If I hadn't, someone could have been hurt—or worse."

"You sacrificed your career for the sake of fellow officers and the public." She squeezed his hands. "That's pretty heroic."

"My fiancée didn't think so."

"You were engaged?" She looked surprised. "Alexis?"

"Yes." He stood and started pacing the room. "Alexis Davidson."

"Pretty name."

"It fit her. She was beautiful." He stopped walking and looked down at her. "I needed a job. When I told her about the one on the force in Kalispell, she said no way she was moving to a two-bit town in backwoods Montana."

"If she loved you, she would have gone anywhere just to be with you."

"Then I guess she didn't." Some detective he was that

he hadn't seen the truth. "It never crossed my mind that I'd lose the career I'd worked my ass off for and the woman I loved because I did the right thing."

Lani shook her head. "I'm sorry she hurt you, but it seems to me you dodged a bullet there."

"How so?"

"That woman was, probably still is, shallow as a cookie sheet if she couldn't see that you're a good man, with character and the courage of his convictions. Then there's that little thing in the marriage vows—for better or worse. The going got tough and she got going." Lani's eyes blazed with anger and disapproval. "She didn't know what she had and didn't deserve you. You're better off without her."

"You think so?" Russ wondered if Lani was as loyal as she seemed.

"I know so. And I'm not sure which is worse—her leaving you or good men who take pride in supporting each other but didn't support one of their own."

"Yeah. I learned the hard way that having someone's back doesn't mean it's okay to lie for them."

Lani went still for just a second then looked up at him. There was a plea in her eyes that said she knew what he was getting at. "Sometimes having someone's back means you can't say anything at all."

The words opened up a hollow feeling in his gut. She wasn't going to tell him why she made him arrest her, or kept him locked up and off the street. Damn it. Now the line was drawn—and Russ had to figure out whether or not he could risk crossing it.

Even for Lani.

Chapter Thirteen

Three days later Lani was working at the Ace in the Hole and fretting because she hadn't seen Russ since he'd dropped her off to pick up her truck. It had been the best of nights and the worst.

She'd felt all gooey and warm and intimate and *close*. For just a little while the attraction between them was something more. Something special that had a chance of being more. But then he opened up about the horrible way he was treated while working for the Denver PD. Outrage didn't begin to describe how she felt for him. And he'd endured a double whammy when the woman he loved had dumped him. Alexis. She was an idiot, and there was nothing left to say about her.

Lani knew from personal experience that honest men didn't grow on trees and Russ was that, and so much more. That night he'd taken her to his room at the boardinghouse he'd wanted her as much as she wanted him. Then the other shoe dropped. He'd said having someone's back didn't mean it was okay to lie for them.

She knew he was asking why she'd forced him to arrest her. She couldn't even explain that she'd done it so Anderson wouldn't be hauled off to jail and end up with a police record. That would lead to questions that she couldn't answer and would make her look even worse.

Telling the truth would break her promise to her brother. Refusing to answer would fuel Russ's doubts about her. As he'd said the other night—damned if she did, damned if she didn't.

She'd seen the look in his eyes when she hadn't taken the hint to tell all about her arrest that night. She knew that answers were important to him. Heck, he was a detective, and a case could be made for answers being his life. But this one she had to keep to herself. When he drove her to her truck, they didn't say anything, which kind of said everything.

So here she was, working at the bar and getting her hopes dashed every time the rusty screen door opened and Russ didn't walk in. It was slow right now, the time of the day after the lunch crowd and before the dinner rush. She stacked the few burger baskets and eating utensils in a big plastic tote and dropped them off in the kitchen. Busing tables was busy work and just what she needed if there was even the slightest chance of getting Russ off her mind.

To get ready for the dinner crowd she put napkin-wrapped silverware in booths and on tables. Filling saltshakers and napkin holders also needed to be done. Behind her she heard the screen door open and gave herself a stern warning not to look. Herself didn't pay the least bit of attention and looked anyway, just in time to see Russ walk in with Gage Christensen. The two men took a booth by the front window.

Alrighty, then, she thought. He would have to talk to

her now. It was her job to take his order. So she walked over and did her best to look normal, as if her heart wasn't hammering hard enough to be heard.

She smiled at both men. "Hi, Gage. Russ. How's it going?"

The sheriff took off his hat and set it on the booth bench beside him. "Good."

"Glad to hear that."

"It would be better if you and Russ could find out who spiked that wedding punch."

"Yeah." She looked at the detective. "It's pretty hard to figure out who's responsible when there are zero clues. So you shouldn't feel bad." About the case, she thought.

"I don't. Sometimes you get what you need." He met her gaze, and there was a disappointed look in his eyes. "And sometimes you don't."

Right now she wished he would cut her a little slack. More than anything she needed to talk to him, but not in front of Gage.

"So what can I get you two?" She pulled a pad and pencil out of her jeans pocket."

"Burger and coffee for me," Gage said.

"Isn't it a little late for lunch?"

"We've been busy. Going over all the information Russ gathered in the investigation."

Something squeezed in her chest at the reminder that Russ was temporary, and his allotted time was soon coming to an end. "Do you want fries or a side salad with your burger?"

Gage's expression was wry. "Salad? Seriously? Have you been talking to my wife? She thinks I need to eat more healthy food, and salad is at the top of her list. How can a man do a hard day's work when he eats the equivalent of grass?"

"This is where I point out that cows and horses kind of

do that, and they work pretty hard." Lani tapped her pencil against the pad.

"It's a conspiracy, right?" Gage teased. "All you women stick together."

"Darn right." She glanced at Russ, who'd been really quiet. "You're going to leave him blowing in the wind on this?"

One corner of his mouth curved up. "At the risk of mixing metaphors, he dug the hole. All he had to say was 'I'll take fries.'"

"He's got you there, Gage."

"Two against one. And I thought you were my friend, Russ." He sighed. "Fries it is. But don't rat me out to Lissa."

"It's not carved in stone, but I think discretion in this job is sort of client privilege. Your secret is safe with me." She looked at Russ. "What'll you have?"

"The same."

"Okay. So, I've got two burgers, fries and coffee." When both men nodded she said, "I'll get this going and be back with the coffee."

She took the order to the kitchen, where Rosey was doing the cooking, filling in during this slow time until someone came in to work the evening rush. Lani handed her the piece of paper.

"This is for the sheriff and Russ Campbell." Her boss gave seriously generous portions to law enforcement and US military veterans, so the information was important.

"Coming right up," Rosey said, tossing a couple of thick beef patties on the industrial-sized stove top. She lowered a basket of sliced potatoes into the hot grease then looked over her shoulder and frowned. "You okay, Lani?"

"Yeah."

"Now that I think about it, you've been kind of down the last few days. Not yourself. Are you really okay?"

"Fine."

"That's the code word for man trouble."

"No, it's just—"

"Save it." Rosey flipped the burgers and pulled two red plastic baskets from the shelf above the stove. "I know when a woman is unhappy, and it's all about a man."

She couldn't tell her boss about the problem because it involved Anderson's issue, and he'd said not to talk about it to anyone. But there were concerns that she *could* talk about. "Russ's time here in Rust Creek Falls is almost over."

"Not the end of the world." The other woman grabbed the long handle of the fry basket and pulled it up, hooking the contraption above the grease to drain. "He lives in Boulder Junction, and it's not that far away."

And that's when Lani voiced another something else that had thrown her. "He didn't want to give up his career in Denver and come back to Montana."

"Then why did he?"

"He exposed a corrupt cop on the Denver force, and no one backed him up. Without officer support it became dangerous for him and the general public if he stayed on." She watched Rosey put tomato, lettuce, onion and pickle in the baskets beside the open buns. "So he came home. But what if he decides small-town life doesn't appeal to him after living and working in the big city?"

"Then you go with him if he decides to make a change." Rosey's tone said "duh" but when she looked over, there was sympathy in her eyes. "Life is full of choices. Not all of them are no-brainers."

"Yeah." Lani had voiced the concern because it would break her heart if he moved away. There wasn't a doubt in her mind that if Russ asked, she would follow him anywhere. "I have to get their coffee, then I'll be back for the hamburgers."

"Okay. And, honey?"

She looked over her shoulder. "Yeah?"

"For what it's worth, all those months Russ was coming here? Let's just say it wasn't about the beer."

"Then what?" Lani asked.

"You. It's obvious."

"Not to me. Respectfully, you're wrong, Rosey. He never talked to me."

"I'm not saying it was easy for him to come in. Maybe he didn't want to, but he couldn't help himself. Couldn't stay away from you. And—" Rosey pointed the spatula in Lani's direction "—he couldn't take his eyes off you."

That was before she'd gotten herself arrested then took his keys to keep him from arresting her brother. If only she could tell him why she'd done it. Then he might understand. "Thanks for trying to make me feel better, Rosey."

"Anytime. Hang in there, honey. The course of true love is never smooth sailing. That's what Sam always says. He likes to talk in navy SEAL metaphors."

Lani really hoped this wasn't love. She didn't know what to call it, but she didn't want to even think the L-word.

She poured coffee into two mugs and delivered them to the lawmen. Both took it black. A few minutes later she brought their food and said, "Let me know if you need anything else."

Then she turned her back and occupied herself with busy work while stealing looks at Russ. A couple of times she was almost sure he was looking at her, too. That was all she needed to make up her mind to talk to him alone if she got the chance.

Just after finishing his food, Gage pulled out his cell phone and answered it. She was too far away to hear what he said, but he grabbed his hat and slid out of the booth before ending the call. He reached into the pocket of his uniform pants to pull out money, but Russ put up his hand. Lani didn't have to hear what they were saying. This was men dealing with who would get the check. Women usually split it however many ways down to the half cent. The guys were more macho and straightforward, and that wasn't altogether a bad thing.

She waited until Gage was gone to bring over the bill and set it on the table. "No rush on that. Can I get you more coffee?"

"No, thanks." That was his cop voice, the one without a drop of emotion and designed to make a person believe God gave him extraordinary good looks at the expense of a sense of humor. "I have to get going."

"Back to the sheriff's office?"

"Things to catch up on." That didn't answer the question.

"Well, things will just have to wait a few minutes." The place was practically empty, and this was as good a time as any to talk, so Lani sat in the space Gage had vacated moments before. "I have a question."

"Okay."

His expression wasn't as agreeable as his response. A woman couldn't have three brothers and not know when a man would rather eat glass than have a conversation. Tough.

Lani folded her hands together and settled them in her lap. "What's bugging you? And don't pretend you don't know what I mean. You acted weird the other night when we left the boardinghouse, and I'm pretty sure it had nothing to do with Melba Strickland's house rules. You've got the same look on your face now, so it's a good bet that nothing's changed."

"You don't want to have this conversation, Lani."

"If I didn't, I wouldn't have asked." Her heart was pounding hard. "So, what's wrong?"

"Okay." He toyed with the handle on his coffee mug. "I keep going back to that night. The Fourth of July. You made it impossible for me not to arrest you. I need to know why."

"And I told you that I can't tell you. But it has nothing to do with—"

He reached for the check. "We're done here."

"Wait, Russ. Please try to understand. I have a very good reason for what I did. Ask anyone and they'll tell you that I'm an upstanding person who follows the rules." She thought for a moment. "Except maybe at the boardinghouse."

He didn't smile. "I know all of that. But honesty is the cornerstone of trust, and I can't overlook the fact that there's something you're not telling me."

"This thing isn't mine to tell. Haven't you ever made a promise to someone? A vow to keep something to yourself?"

"Yes. And my word is important to me. But when laws are broken, everything changes."

She remembered the look on his face when he told her about the woman he'd loved not supporting him at probably the lowest point in his life. A violation of his trust that left a mark. It was making him dig in and not give an inch now.

"This isn't entirely about obeying the law or honesty, is it, Russ?"

His mouth pulled tight, and a muscle jerked in his jaw. "I was blindsided once. It's not a feeling I ever want to experience again. That cost me my career. Now I have a second chance, and I'm not going to blow it."

Before she could collect her thoughts and tell him she was nothing like his ex, he'd tossed some bills on the table.

"Keep the change," he said. Without another word, he stood up and walked out the door without looking back even once.

Well, she had more to say. And if Russ thought that was the end of this, he didn't really know her at all.

* * *

After leaving Lani at the bar, Russ went back to the sheriff's office to go over his eyewitness interviews for the investigation. Maybe there was something he'd missed, a slip of the tongue to warrant another conversation. To the best of his knowledge, he'd talked to everyone who was at the park that night, except Old Man Sullivan, who disappeared from town after losing his ranch to Brad Crawford during the poker game at the Ace in the Hole. Without a lead, there was nothing left to go on, and Russ was damned frustrated. So he went back to Strickland's Boarding House.

After pacing his room for a while, he yanked his duffel out of the closet and set it on the bed then pulled jeans and shirts from the dresser. His assignment wasn't over for a couple of days yet but since he had the evening ahead of him, he might as well pack. He had nowhere to go, nothing to do and no one to do it with. Getting ready to leave Rust Creek Falls might take his mind off Lani and how much he wanted to see her, take her to bed again. If only he could trust her…

There was a knock on the door, and the sound was almost as startling as a gunshot. He hated himself for it, but couldn't help hoping Lani had changed her mind about holding back her secret.

He opened the door and was almost as surprised by who was there—Melba and Old Gene Strickland, the boardinghouse owners.

"Hi," he said.

"Hello, Mr. Campbell." Melba was somewhere in her late seventies or early eighties, but didn't look a day over sixty-five.

"I thought you were going to call me Russ."

"If it's all the same to you, we prefer to address our

boarders more formally." Old Gene cleared his throat. "Friendly but not friends, if you know what I mean."

Not really, Russ thought. But he'd handled characters more eccentric than these two. "I'm okay with that."

"Good. Sensible. Young folks today have no boundaries. They walk around with those dang machines in their hands and don't look either way before crossing the street."

"My husband doesn't like smartphones," Melba shared.

"Stupid name," the old man grumbled. "If you ask me, the world would be better off without everyone sharing everything they do and think with everyone else on the planet."

"Change isn't easy," his wife sympathized.

"That's for sure," Gene agreed. "Computer nerds call it updates. Keep trying to make things better and just confuse the dickens out of folks. Should just leave well enough alone."

"He's still mad about Words with Friends. Gene loves to play Scrabble. Keeps his mind sharp," Melba explained. "So one of our granddaughters set him up and got him started. Then some genius decided it needed to be updated. The contraption wouldn't let him play until it was."

"The thing is," Gene said, "I couldn't figure out how to do it and got so aggravated I nearly chucked that machine from here to Kalispell."

"Finally, I started fiddling with it and somehow got a phone call from a nice young man who helped. Now Gene is playing again."

"Until the next time they want to make it better." The older man shook his head.

"Let's not borrow trouble," Melba advised.

"All this virtual stuff… There was nothing virtual about anything in the old days. You could see it, touch it, smell it. Hard work was hard work. Men were men, not telephone operators. And women had babies and took care of their families. They didn't have a badge and a gun and drive a fire truck."

"You're a bit of a chauvinist, dear," his wife told him affectionately.

Russ was beginning to wonder if they needed him and if not, why they'd come to see him at all.

"Was there something you wanted?" he asked. "Maybe you'd like to come in?"

"No, Mr. Campbell. We don't want to invade your privacy. This won't take long." Melba's voice took on a stern quality. "It's come to my attention that you had a visitor in your room the other night." She raised an eyebrow, waiting for him to confirm what she obviously already knew.

But how did she know? Was the room bugged? Did they have video surveillance? She continued to wait for him to fill the silence, and he wondered if she'd ever done criminal interrogations. But he wasn't a rookie and stared right back at her without saying anything.

Melba cleared her throat. "This is a boardinghouse, not a brothel, Mr. Campbell. I don't approve of premarital sex. If Lani Dalton visits you in this room, she best have your ring on her finger when she does it."

"Lani? How did you—" Damn. Melba was good. Drop a name, make it personal, emotions took over and something slips out.

Satisfaction sliced through the older woman's eyes. "I have a business reputation to maintain. It's my job to know what goes on under my roof."

"You do know that my stay here is almost over," he said, neither confirming nor denying.

"Of course. It's my responsibility to know," she said. "That still doesn't make it all right to break the rules. If we look the other way for you, standards go out the window. You're a policeman, Mr. Campbell. You know about enforcing rules."

"She's pretty set on this," Gene said.

Russ swore there was man-to-man sympathy in the old guy's eyes, but not enough to take on the little woman. There was no point in protesting, since he would be gone soon. And judging by the anger and hurt in Lani's eyes earlier, there was no chance she would step foot in this room again. He missed her already.

"I understand," he lied. "I guarantee no woman will be in this room while I still occupy it."

"I'm glad to hear that." Melba smiled. "Thank you for your understanding, Mr. Campbell."

Funny, Russ thought, how she could go from stubborn to sweet in a heartbeat. He would bet she was a formidable mother, loving and warm unless forced to take a hard line with her children.

"You're welcome," he said. "Don't worry about me—"

"Mrs. Strickland. Mr. Strickland." The voice in the hall sounded just like Lani. She appeared in the doorway and smiled at the older couple. "How are you?"

"Hello, Lani, dear," Melba said. "Gene and I are fine. How are you?"

"Good." She glanced at him, and the shadows visible in her eyes said that she wasn't fine at all. "I'm here to see Russ. Just to talk."

"If a pretty girl came to see me, I wouldn't be thinking about talking," Gene mumbled.

"Be that as it may," Melba said to Lani, "we know you were here the other night and were just discussing the situation with Mr. Campbell. Remember that respectability and reputation are important."

"Yes, ma'am. I'm the soul of propriety. Honest and true blue." She gave him a pointed look.

"All right, then. Can't do any more. It isn't against the law, so no one can be arrested." But the older woman gave each of them a look then settled her gaze on Lani. "You're on your honor. Remember us to your parents, dear."

"Yes, ma'am."

"If I were you," Gene said to Russ, "I'd give her a ring."

"Come along," Melba said to her husband. They started to walk away but she turned back and asked, "Any progress on your investigation into that unfortunate spiked punch incident on the Fourth of July?"

"No, ma'am. I've followed every lead, questioned everyone there that night who's still in town. Didn't turn up anything."

"Too bad." The older woman moved down the hall with Old Gene following.

And then he was alone with Lani.

"What did they say?" she asked.

"That they didn't want to invade my privacy," he answered wryly. "Just before invading it."

"They mean well." She shrugged.

He was still standing in the doorway, looking at her in the hall. "I'm surprised to see you."

"I took a shot."

Russ wanted to hold her so bad it hurt deep down inside. He wanted to kiss her and break Melba Strickland's ridiculous rule. But he held back. "A shot at what?"

She tucked a long shiny strand of hair behind her ear. "Coming to talk to you. It felt like there was more to say."

"That's up to you." And there it was. The elephant in the room. The secret she wouldn't give up.

"Can I come in?"

"Sure." He stepped aside and she walked past, the scent of her burrowing inside to warm his blood. He closed the door then turned and saw her staring at the bed, more specifically, the duffel with clothes beside it.

"You're leaving?"

It sounded like an accusation, a breach of trust. Coming

from her that was ironic and got his defenses up. "I was only ever staying for a couple of weeks."

"But your time isn't up yet," she protested.

"It will be soon."

"So you're packing early." Her tone was flat. "I guess that means you can't wait to get back to your regularly scheduled life."

Truthfully, his life was a mess. He'd tried so hard to not let Lani matter to him, and now he knew it was going to rip him up to say goodbye. When he walked away from this assignment and this woman, all he'd have would be his job with Kalispell PD and it was safer to focus on that, on his career. But dammit, right this second, while he was close enough to feel the heat of her body, smell the scent of her skin, he couldn't imagine being alone, and the thought gave him a hollow feeling in the pit of his stomach. He'd better get used to it.

"Cases in Kalispell have probably been piling up on my desk while I've been gone. I'm going to be busy when I go back."

"So you're telling me you won't be coming to Rust Creek Falls? To fill in when the sheriff asks?"

"No." Because seeing her with no way to bridge the divide between them would probably kill him. But she'd come here to say something, and the least he could do was hear her out. "What did you want to talk about?"

"Are you even going to say goodbye?" There was a world of hurt in her eyes. "Never mind. It's not important now. Sorry I bothered you. Hope I didn't get you in trouble with the Stricklands."

"You didn't bother me. Lani, I—" He stopped when she opened the door.

"Bye, Russ," she said without turning around.

And then he was alone, and not even the fragrance of

her perfume lingering in the room could stop the empty feeling from widening inside him.

He kicked himself for not being able to get past his past. Lani said she wasn't at liberty to explain her behavior that night, and if he hadn't been sucker punched at the worst time in his life, her refusal probably wouldn't matter. He could overlook it. But even though all his instincts were telling him that Lani was as loyal and honest as she was beautiful, he kept tripping over his doubts. And as much as he wanted to go after her, Lani's secret was standing in the way.

Chapter Fourteen

On the way to the ranch the next morning Lani was tired. It tended to happen when you couldn't sleep, and that was Russ Campbell's fault. If he hadn't told her last night that he wouldn't be back to Rust Creek Falls, she'd have slept like a baby. But he did tell her, and he meant it. Tears she'd been fighting since walking away from the boarding-house filled her eyes. And that made her mad. He wouldn't take another chance on a relationship, and she wanted five minutes alone with his ex. It would feel good to give that woman a piece of her mind and a stern lecture about loyalty and support. She certainly hadn't loved him.

Not in Lani's book anyway. You couldn't be in love with someone and abandon them when they needed you most. She was pretty sure it wasn't her Russ distrusted as much as it was love. He was just looking for an excuse to push her away.

She parked her truck in front of Anderson's house and went inside to make coffee. The pot was already brewing, and she peeked into the living room and remembered the day she'd defended Russ when he took on Travis and Anderson. The room blurred as moisture filled her eyes.

"Morning, Lani." Anderson walked into his kitchen.

"Hey." She hadn't heard him approach and needed a minute to compose herself. She didn't want him to see her upset. "How are you?"

"Good." He moved closer and reached past her into the cupboard to get a mug. "We have to check the fences on the south edge of the ranch. Winter's coming."

In so many ways, she thought, a cold feeling settling around her heart. She brushed a rogue tear from her cheek and cleared her throat. "Okay. I'll take care of it."

"I've got Travis riding fence on the north side of the property."

"Right." She sniffled and still didn't look at her brother. She couldn't because he would know she was upset and grill her for answers she didn't want to give him.

"Are you okay, Lani?" There was concern in his voice.

"Sure." She went to the refrigerator and got out the cream then pulled the box of sweetener that he kept there for her out of the cupboard. "Why?"

"You're acting weird."

"So what else is new?" She was trying to act as if nothing was wrong, and it took a lot of energy she didn't have.

"You keep sniffling. Are you catching a cold?"

"Allergies," she said.

"Since when? I've known you all your life, and you never had allergies before."

"I've read that a person can develop them later in life. It happens." She was going to lose it and didn't want him to be here when she did. "You should go saddle up and get to work."

"Since when are you the boss?"

"It's getting late. You should go."

"Yeah, you're right. And I'll do that as soon as you turn around and look at me."

Damn. Why couldn't he be like most men and not notice that her attitude was off? No way she could get out of it, so she plastered on a smile and faced him. Anderson looked suspicious as he studied her for a moment.

A muscle jerked in his jaw. "You've been crying."

"I'm not a crier. You know that—" Of all people he knew that wasn't true. He'd held her the last time she cried over a man.

"Trust me on this, Lani. You're not a very good liar."

It was the sympathetic look in his eyes that finally did her in. She put her hands over her face and started to cry for real.

"Come here, kid." Anderson pulled her into his arms. "What's wrong? Whoever it is, whatever it is, I'll beat them up for you."

Dear God, his white-knight complex was what got her into this in the first place. He'd hit Skip Webster for punching Travis when he wasn't looking. "I...I don't want to talk about it."

"Don't care what you want, sis." He patted her back. "If you don't tell me what's going on, I'll have to find out on my own. And I'll start with Russ Campbell."

"No!" She pulled away and brushed at the wetness on her cheeks. "Why would you talk to him?"

"Because you haven't blubbered like this since that no-good, sweet-talking liar Jason broke your heart. This is man trouble, and he's the man you've been seeing."

"That doesn't mean this is about him. I don't want to talk about this, Anderson. It's not important."

"It's important if you're upset." His expression was hard, firm. "I know you, little sister, and you don't feel sorry for yourself as a rule. You'll feel better if you talk about what's bothering you."

Not if it made him feel bad. And he would. Because the secret she was keeping belonged to him. She knew he had his reasons for wanting it this way, and she respected whatever they were. Russ Campbell wasn't his problem, he was hers.

"I'll get over it." She sniffled, rubbed her eyes then did her best to smile. "See? All gone."

"In a pig's eye." Anderson's blue eyes flashed with anger. "Okay. That does it. I think I'll just go over to Strickland's Boarding House and find out what the heck is going on between the two of you." He turned toward the doorway that would lead him outside where his truck was parked.

Lani couldn't afford to call his bluff. If he really did see Russ, there might be punches thrown, and everything she'd gone through the night of the Fourth of July would be for nothing. And she'd have a broken heart on top of it.

"Wait. I'll tell you."

He turned around and poured himself a cup of coffee then leaned back against the countertop. "Start talking."

"I fell for Russ Campbell, and he's leaving town."

"That's not unexpected. His assignment was temporary."

"I know. See? I told you it was nothing."

Anderson took a sip of coffee from his heavy mug. "There's more, right? There has to be. You're not one to overreact like this."

"He's gone for good."

"He works in Kalispell and has a house in Boulder Junction. It's not like that's on the moon. You can go see him." Her brother had the look of a man who was sorry he'd started this conversation. "And the sheriff hasn't hired a new deputy yet, so he'll be back to help out just like before."

"He told me his workload has been piling up and he won't be back. Translation—he's just not that into me. Going after him would make me look just as pathetic as begging him to stay. It's déjà vu. Apparently, I'm not the kind of woman a man sticks around for."

Anderson set his mug on the counter then rubbed a hand across his neck. "I don't get it. Word all over town is that you've got him hooked."

"Not so much." She didn't say more. No need to tell him their relationship had been up and down. That it started with sex in a jail cell, turned into a cover for working on the investigation then ended with sex in his boardinghouse room.

Anderson stared at her for several moments, and then the light went on in his eyes. "This is about that night in the park. When he arrested you."

"Yes." She should have known eventually he would put two and two together. "I'm not very good at pretending. He knows I had a reason for getting him to take me in."

"A distraction," Anderson said grimly. "So he wouldn't arrest me."

She nodded. "He doesn't trust me."

"You should have just told him you did it to keep me out of jail and left it at that."

"He's a detective, Anderson. He wouldn't have bought the family-loyalty thing. He'd dig deeper to find out why it was so important that you not be arrested and have a black mark on your record." She sighed. "With your custody issue pending, it wasn't a chance you could afford to take."

"I love you for what you did." He smiled, but it faded fast. "But the promise you made to me is costing you the happiness you deserve." Her brother made a fist and slammed it on the counter.

"It's complicated. And one way to look at it is if he can't trust me, believe that I had a good reason for not telling him, and that I'm not breaking any laws, maybe I dodged a bullet and this is for the best."

"You don't really believe that," he said.

"I might after a while."

He closed his eyes for a moment and shook his head. "This is my fault. I never should have made you promise. Better yet, I never should have told you about my personal problem in the first place."

"No. I'm glad you did." She sniffled and put her hand on his arm. "It's a heavy burden to carry alone. I just wish—"

"What?" He frowned when a tear rolled down her cheek.

"I wish Russ didn't have baggage that makes him not want to take a chance on me, on us."

The tears started up again, and Anderson pulled her in for a hug. "I'm so sorry, Lani."

"Me, too."

"It will be all right."

"I know." She grabbed a tissue from the box sitting on his counter and blew her nose. "I'm made of stern stuff. It takes a lot more than this to get me down."

"We'll figure out something."

How she loved her big brother for wanting to fix what was wrong with her life. But there was nothing he could do. His child was involved, and that had to be his priority.

"I can take care of myself," she assured him. "I'll be fine."

But she didn't believe that. Not really. She was in love with Russ, and it had taken losing him to bring that realization into sharp focus. She had a feeling nothing would be all right ever again.

Several days after Lani had come to see him in his room Russ was at the sheriff's office late into the evening on his last day of the spiked punch assignment. There were loose ends and paperwork to tie up before he left Rust Creek Falls for good. He was writing his final report on the investigation, and it was taking a lot longer than reports usually did. Everything in the account of his findings reminded him of Lani.

Riding with her to the falls for strategy planning. The interview with Jordyn Leigh Cates Clifton that resulted in their dating cover story to explain spending time together. When she went rogue and had a beer with Brad Crawford before she ruled him out as a suspect but ended up in Russ's bed. That hadn't moved the investigation forward, but it was a night he would never forget.

He'd known better than to make love to her but hadn't been able to help himself. But that was no excuse. It was selfish to keep seeing her when he couldn't take a chance and had no intention of committing. He didn't trust any woman to be there for him, so what was the point?

Still, he kept seeing the look in Lani's eyes when he'd said he wouldn't be coming back to Rust Creek Falls. She'd felt used, and he couldn't blame her. He hated himself for hurting her, and it was all he could do to stop himself from going to her.

But she deserved better than that.

The front door opened and the sheriff walked in. "I thought you might still be here."

"I didn't expect to see you. Thought you'd gone home to your wife." Russ envied his friend. Gage was good at his job, and there was no question that the man was devoted to the town. But Russ always got the feeling that a part of him was only filling time until he could be with the woman he loved. "Why did you come back?"

"This is your last night. I thought we might go get a beer at the Ace in the Hole."

"I have to finish this report." Russ was stalling because the thing was finally done. The truth was that if he saw Lani, his resolve to put Rust Creek Falls in his rearview mirror might weaken. He refused to be made a fool of again, and the only way to be sure it wouldn't happen was to keep her out. And speaking of the investigation report… "I'm sorry I let you down."

"You didn't." Gage obviously understood what he was referring to. He moved closer and rested a hip on the edge of the desk. "Why would you say that?"

"We still don't know who spiked the punch." He shrugged. "That's a complete failure to achieve the objective for which I was hired."

"Not from my perspective," Gage said. "Your interviews ruled out pretty much everyone who lives here in Rust Creek Falls, so we know who didn't do it. On top of that, there hasn't been another incident. My theory is that this was random mischief, probably by someone who was passing through town. Folks are starting to breathe easier now. Not so skittish. And that's thanks to you."

"Still, not knowing who did it is like a rock in my boot. I really wanted to catch the person responsible."

"Whoever did it was smart. They covered their tracks and got lucky that no one witnessed it. But the exhaustive investigation sent a warning that misconduct won't be tolerated. My gut is telling me there's no further threat."

"I agree." Russ printed out a hard copy of the report for the file along with his notes. Then he saved everything on the hard drive and shut down the computer he'd been using.

"So, about that beer…" There was a definite challenge in Gage's eyes.

"I'm all packed up. Ready to head out." Russ let the thought hang between them.

"I've never known you to turn down a beer."

"Always a first time. Been here in Rust Creek Falls a long time. I really should get back." Back to an empty house and a life that was nothing but work. No Lani. No sassy lady with a quick wit and sunny smile waiting for him at the end of a hard day. He was going to miss her. But he'd been lonely before and could learn to deal with it again.

"I think you're avoiding her." Gage folded his arms over his chest. A challenge if there ever was one.

"You're wrong." Russ didn't need to clarify who *her* was.

"I don't think so. You're the detective, but I keep the peace here in Rust Creek. I'm an officer of the law, too, and powers of observation go with the territory."

"What's your point?"

"A blind man could see there's something simmering between you and Lani. And there has been ever since that night you were locked up together."

Because she stole my keys, Russ thought. Funny, he didn't mind so much anymore that she had. What happened after that was another fine memory he could take with him.

Gage looked thoughtful. "Come to think of it, even before that night there was something. More than once I was at the bar with you. I saw the way you looked at her, and she was looking back just as hard. I was always surprised that you never did anything about it."

"I got burned once."

"Figured as much. But still… You didn't make a move."

"Like what?"

"Like asking her out, Sherlock," Gage said.

Russ thought he'd covered his feelings pretty well, but now Gage's detective senses were apparently tingling. "Is that why you suggested Lani could help with the investigation? Were you playing matchmaker?"

"Wish I'd thought of it." But there was a self-satisfied look in Gage's eyes. "But she really does know everyone in town."

"You were playing Cupid? Trust me, it's not a good look for you," he snapped.

Russ could have refused to work with her, but took the suggestion because this was Gage's town, and he understood it. Maybe part of him jumped at it for an excuse to see her. But after spending so much time with Lani, leaving her was going to rip his heart out.

"What the hell were you thinking, Gage?"

His friend's eyes narrowed. Instead of answering the question, he asked, "What the hell did you do that night in the cell?"

Russ recognized the brotherly protectiveness in the sheriff's attitude and respected it. But before he could frame a response, Lani's actual big brother walked into the office.

Anderson Dalton stopped in front of the desk. "Gage."

"Nice to see you, Anderson. What brings you in here?"

"I need to talk to Detective Campbell." He looked at both of them before his steely-eyed gaze settled on Russ. "Alone, if that's all right."

"No problem. I've got paperwork." He straightened then went into his private office and closed the door.

The angry look on the other man's face made Russ stand, ready for anything. He figured Gage had seen it, too, and that's why he didn't leave the office.

"Nice to see you, Anderson."

"I doubt that. We need to talk."

There was only one thing they had in common. "About Lani."

"You made my sister cry. She doesn't do that very often, and it makes me want to tear you apart."

Russ wouldn't mind mixing it up. The other man was about his weight and height but didn't have the kind of training a cop gets. But he understood where Anderson was coming from. Having a sister was a responsibility, and Russ *had* hurt Lani.

"So what's stopping you?"

"For one thing, my sister wouldn't like it." Anderson almost smiled.

"What else?"

"I want all the facts out in the open."

"What might those be?" Russ asked.

"This misunderstanding between you and Lani is my fault."

That was a surprise. Russ stared at him. "Go on."

"The night of the wedding reception I was drunk from whatever was in that damn punch."

"You and most of the town," Russ said. "What's your point?"

"I decked Skip Webster because he sucker punched my brother. It was pretty obvious that you were headed over to slap cuffs on me. Lani saw what was going on and jumped in the fountain to distract you from arresting me."

"Why would she risk going to jail?" Russ demanded. "Charges would probably have been dropped, especially when it turned out that the punch was tampered with."

"In the moment no one knew that or was thinking about it." The other man's expression hardened. "Lani was only thinking about me, about the fact that it would put a black mark on my record."

"So what if there was an arrest? It wouldn't be that big a deal."

"It could be for me." Anderson let out a long breath then met his gaze. "Recently I learned I have a child I never knew about. I'm going to file for custody, and we both know the family court system favors mothers, so any ding on my record would affect my chances of prevailing in court."

"So why didn't Lani just tell me that?"

"I made her promise not to tell anyone." His blue eyes blazed, evidence that he was angry and frustrated with himself and the whole situation.

"Not even your family? Your father's an attorney." A good one, according to Lani. She'd made that clear to Russ when they'd spent the night behind bars.

"The last thing I want is to involve my family." Anderson rubbed a hand over his face and suddenly looked tired. "It would just hurt them to know there's a grandchild out there and they never knew. It's my problem, and I'll deal with it. I'll give them the facts when the case is resolved."

"And Lani is the only one who knows?"

He nodded. "And now you."

"Why are you telling me?"

"Because when Lani makes a promise, she keeps it. End of story. She's so loyal, she would jeopardize her own future in order to keep a vow she made to me. I couldn't live with myself if I was to blame for her unhappiness."

Russ felt as if he was in a shoot-out, with bullets coming from every direction. He was having trouble wrapping his brain around all this. "What are you saying?"

"God knows why, but Lani loves you, and this secret is coming between you. She says you've got your reasons. But personally I think it's an excuse to play around then duck and run when things get complicated. An easy way out."

"You're wrong." Anger pulsed through Russ. "I know what it feels like when a woman you thought you knew throws you under the bus when the going gets tough. Your career is going full-speed backward and just when you think things can't get worse, she hands back the ring and proves you wrong."

"So you got dumped." Anderson clenched his jaw and a muscle jerked. "Detective, you don't know what personal betrayal is until you find out a woman had your baby and for years never bothered to let you know."

He was right. Holy crap, Russ thought. That was pretty low. With absolute certainty he knew that Lani would never do that. With that realization came another one. He'd acted like an ass.

"Okay, Anderson. You win."

"Believe me, I'd give anything not to come out on top in this situation. But it got to me," he said. "And I needed to tell someone. Lani was there for me, and I don't know if I could get through this without her. But there's no way I'm going to let my problem cost her."

"I appreciate you telling me." Russ felt a weight lift from his shoulders and realized those weren't just words. He really meant what he said.

Anderson nodded. "I'd appreciate it if you'd keep what I just told you confidential."

"No one will hear it from me." Russ held out his hand, and Anderson took it.

He respected what this man was going through and his overriding concern to protect his family. And Lani was helping him. She was so committed to keeping her word and having her brother's back that she was willing to let Russ think the worst of her.

That's what the pain in her eyes was all about, and he hated himself even more for putting it there. He knew now what she'd meant about not saying anything also being a way to have someone's back. He was too blinded by bitterness from his past to see her pure heart. There must be a way to fix what he'd done.

"Thanks, Russ."

"No problem." He watched Anderson walk outside and get in his truck parked at the curb.

Gage must have heard him leave because he came out of his office. "So what was that all about?"

"I could tell you, but then I'd have to kill you." Russ dragged a hand through his hair.

"Lani." Gage's tone said *gotcha.* He rested his hands on his hips. "And before you risk your detective shield by asking why I would say that, I'll just give you the facts."

"Please do." Russ folded his arms over his chest and waited.

"If Anderson was here to report stolen cattle or inform us that a crime was committed, you would have happily shared that information. But he's Lani's brother, so the logical conclusion is that he came to confront you about your relationship with his sister." Gage stopped and made a great show of examining Russ's face.

"What?"

"I was just wondering where the black eye is. The fat lip."

"And why would that be?"

"Because you courted his sister, and now you're running out on her."

Russ opened his mouth to dispute that assessment then realized there was a lot of truth in it. And it was pointless to ask how he knew all this. Rust Creek Falls had a gossip mill that was second to none.

"Let's just say that Anderson is a very civilized man."

"So you're really not going to tell me what he said?"

"It's classified." Russ grinned at his friend's obvious frustration. "Lissa will just have to find something else to blog about."

"I thought we were friends," Gage commented.

"We are."

"Good. Then in the spirit of friendship I'm going to let you know that Lani is working tonight." Gage met his gaze. "Go to the Ace in the Hole and buy your own damn beer."

"Understood."

Russ grabbed his leather jacket off the chair and headed out the door. It was always good when a friend's advice coincided with your own plan of action.

Chapter Fifteen

"Hey, Lani, can I get a glass of wine for Kathy?"

"Sure thing, Wes. What'll you have?"

"Beer."

She opened a bottle of Chardonnay and poured some into a wineglass, got a longneck from the small refrigerator below the bar then set both on cocktail napkins in front of Wes Eggleston and his pretty brunette wife.

"Thanks," they both said together.

"It's nice to see you two in here. Where's that adorable little girl of yours?"

"My mom is keeping Chloe overnight." Kathy smiled at her husband. "This is date night."

"Oh?"

"We went to counseling," Wes explained.

Lani remembered talking to him about it just a few weeks ago, the day Russ had come in to ask for her help in solving the town mystery. Fortunately, things worked out better for this couple than they had for her.

"How did that go?" she asked. "Since you're here I'm guessing it was positive?"

"It wasn't as bad as I expected." He glanced at his wife. "We have some things to work through. Make our relationship stronger."

"And she suggested we make an effort to do something alone at least once or twice a month." Kathy took a sip of wine. "And I have to say it's working for me."

"That's great," Lani said.

"I love my daughter so much," she said, "but it sure is nice to have a break. Quiet time just for Wes and me."

"I never knew she felt that way," her husband said. He looked at the woman beside him with a lot of love in his eyes. "Communication is one of the things we're going to work on. Sometimes that means just listening."

"Makes sense," Lani said. "I'm so glad for you guys. This is really wonderful."

"Hey, Lani—"

She glanced over her shoulder and saw a cowboy at the far end of the bar, his arm around a tiny blonde. He was trying to get her attention. Holding up a hand, she signaled that she'd heard then said to the young couple, "Congrats. I'll ring up your drinks when I get a few minutes. Gotta go."

Annie had picked the wrong night to call in sick, Lani thought. The Ace in the Hole was always hopping on Fridays. The dinner rush had slowed but a lot of people were coming in for drinks. And by people she meant couples. They were smiling, laughing and cuddling. The PDAs going on were enough to make her wish they'd all get a room. Fate seemed determined to rub her nose in the fact that she was alone. She'd lost Russ. Although technically she'd never had him, which meant she couldn't really lose him.

Her attitude sucked, but there was no way to take a

timeout and adjust it. *Sue me*, she thought. It was hard to watch couples in love when the night before you'd had your heart handed back with a firm no-thank-you.

She grabbed two beers and handed them to the cowboy and his lady. He gave her a bill and told her to keep the change, so that's what she did. Standing beside the cash register, she surveyed the bar. Almost every stool was taken, and she couldn't see the tables in the main dining area. Just as well. It was probably full of more happy couples for her to envy.

A twosome right in front of her got up after leaving money with their bill. Before she could say boo, the empty stools were taken by her brothers.

"What do you want?" she said.

"Wow." Anderson's eyebrow rose. "If that's the best you can do, your people skills could use some work."

"My skills are just fine, thanks. I don't have to be nice to you."

"Says who?" Travis's eyes twinkled. "I'm telling Rosey."

"Seriously? You'd rat me out?"

"In a hot minute," he said cheerfully. "What are brothers for?"

She put a hand on her hip. "Somewhere I read that brothers teach us you can love someone even though they irritate the crap out of you. Why are you here?"

Lani glanced at Anderson, and he nodded slightly, letting her know that Travis was aware of what happened between her and Russ. So this was a show of family support. It was all she could do not to cover her face and blubber like a baby. Along with so many other wonderful purposes, brothers were there to cheer you up when a man broke your heart.

"You guys are the best." She pointed at each of them. "Don't let that go to your heads, or I'll deny I ever said such a thing."

"My lips are sealed." Travis gave her an evil grin. "Until the next time you get me in trouble with Mom. Then all bets are off."

"We'll see about that. It will go badly for you." She dragged the side of her hand across her neck, the universal sign for cutting his own throat. "What can I get for you troublemakers?"

"Beer," they said together.

"Okay." Lani retrieved two from the fridge and noticed the supply was getting low. She made a mental note to restock as soon as business slowed down a bit. Twisting off the caps, she set the drinks down in front of her brothers. "Cheers."

Travis took a sip. "Speaking of troublemakers… I had no idea you were really sweet on that detective."

"I'll get over it." She knew this was his last night in town, and her heart was breaking.

Rosey chose that moment to join them. Of course she'd heard everything. "I knew there was something bothering you. If these two clueless cowpokes are here to cheer you up, it must be bad. What happened with you and Detective Dreamy?"

There were customers sitting to the right and left of her brothers, and people with drinks in hand filling the open area behind them. All of a sudden it got very quiet, as if everyone in the bar was waiting to hear her answer.

"Well," she started, "things didn't work out."

"That tells me exactly nothing," Rosey informed her. "It didn't work out for you? Or was it him? It makes a difference who the not-working-out part came from."

If there was a God in heaven, Lani thought, the earth would open and swallow her now. She waited, but nothing happened, and her boss was looking as if she expected a response.

She leaned over and whispered, "You know, Rosey, I don't really want to talk about this right now."

"It's all right, honey. This is the best time to get it out. No one is listening."

"What'd you say, Rosey? I can't hear you from back here."

Lani couldn't see who'd said it, but the voice was male. She gave her boss a "really?" look.

"Everyone cares about you, Lani."

"She's right about that," Anderson chimed in.

Lani pressed her lips together and again fought the urge to cry. People being nice to her was both a blessing and curse. If they were mean, she could get mad. For a little while, anger would fill up the empty place inside her. But all this caring threatened to reduce her to a puddle of goo, and that wouldn't be good, since she was trying to keep a low profile over this whole thing. And she knew if she started talking about it, she would cry.

"Please, Rosey, about Russ and me? Let's just call it a draw."

Russ wasn't the bad guy. She wasn't enough for him. She wasn't the one he wanted enough to take a chance with. And her heart cracked a little more when she thought about him being alone.

"That means it was him," Rosey said.

"No. It's just one of those things," Lani answered.

There was a murmur from the crowd, and Anderson glanced over his shoulder at someone. There was an odd expression on his face when he said, "Stop protecting him, Lani. He doesn't deserve it."

"It's not about being deserving." She stared at her brother, who'd gone all negative and intense, which wasn't like Anderson at all. "A person is entitled to their feelings. You can't force something that isn't there."

"You're too good for Russ Campbell," Anderson continued. "He's a fool to let you get away. Someday he'll regret his bonehead move."

Lani blinked at him. Something was wrong. She knew he'd come to the bar during her shift in a show of family solidarity and support. But it wasn't like him to trash-talk publicly like this. She glanced at Rosey, who was staring out into the crowd around the bar.

"You're one of the most open-minded people I know. And a good judge of character. Will you please talk some sense into my brother?"

"Can't," her boss said.

"Why not?"

"He's right. I never knew what you saw in that outsider anyway."

"Right on," someone said. "Didn't trust him at all."

"Travis? A little help." Lani was hoping for backup.

"Don't look at me. I can't say Anderson is wrong. The sheriff hired him, but I was never all in on that." Her brother shrugged.

"I can't believe this," she said.

"He's a snoop and a spy." That was Skip Webster, aka the sucker-punching weasel. "Asking questions. Insinuating a guy's guilty when he's not."

Lani thought he had some nerve criticizing Russ. After all, he was the one who'd started the fight on the Fourth of July. That guy was the reason she'd gotten herself arrested in the first place. Part of her wanted to thank him because otherwise she wouldn't have some wonderful memories of Russ. The other part wanted to call him out for being a hypocritical jerk. The other part won and she snapped.

"Stop it, all of you. I can't believe what I'm hearing. Did someone spike your drinks again? Because this isn't the way Rust Creek Falls folks act. How ungrateful you are! The only thing he's guilty of is trying to keep you all safe. And this is the thanks he gets." She glared at everyone in general and Skip Webster in particular. "You could take a lesson from Russ Campbell, you Neanderthal twit. That man is good and kind. Loyal and upstanding. He deserves your thanks for putting his life on hold. And the only thing he wanted was to help this town. You should be ashamed of yourselves. God knows I'm ashamed of you."

"And you're in love with him," Rosey said as if she'd known it all along.

The time for discretion had passed, Lani realized. She didn't care who was there, who knew how she felt. She stared at her boss and said, "Yes. I'm in love with him. So there. Now the whole town knows, and I don't give a flying fig."

There was movement in the crowd near the bar, and everyone was whispering as they parted to let someone through. When she looked to see what was going on, Russ was standing in front of her.

"Hi, Lani."

Her heart stuttered. "Russ… I didn't see you there."

Russ wanted to jump over the bar and pull her into his arms and never let her go. He'd almost been stupid enough to walk away from her, from the best thing that ever happened to him, without trying. Without telling her how he felt.

"I know you didn't see me," he said to her. "But Anderson did. That's why he was dumping on me."

"Anderson?" Her eyes went wide as she snapped a look at her brother.

"It's true," he admitted. "Rosey, too."

"That's right," the older woman said.

Lani looked at first one then the other, clearly astonished that they would publicly put him down. "But why?"

Russ knew the answer to that one but let her brother respond.

"Even though you're ticked off at him right now, I

knew you'd defend him. Because you always do the right thing, no matter what. That's just the way you roll." Anderson looked at Russ, daring him not to blow this opportunity. "I thought you should know just how special my sister is."

"I knew it before I walked in the door." Russ nodded his thanks. "Someday I hope you meet a woman even half as remarkable."

"I'm done looking." Anderson's vow was laced with the bitterness of his betrayal.

"I thought I was done, too." Russ figured it was a waste of breath to try to change the other man's mind. No one could have convinced him that he would ever meet a woman as beautiful on the inside as she was on the outside.

A woman he could count on.

Travis was watching the exchange with an expression that was equal parts amusement and confusion. "Well, chap my hide and slap me silly."

"Maybe later." Russ looked at Lani, hoping he could undo the damage he'd done. "Lani, we need to talk—"

She shook her head and backed away from the edge of the bar. "Rosey, I'm taking a break now."

"Take as long as you need, honey," her boss said. "I've got this."

As an officer of the law, Russ couldn't say that he always got his man, but he'd be damned if he was going to lose this woman. Lani quickly moved to the end of the bar and flipped back the top to make her escape. But Russ was waiting for her. Blocking her exit. She tried to pass but he didn't move.

"Let me pass," she ordered.

"Not until you hear me out."

"You've already said more than I want to hear." She tried to maneuver around him, but he sidestepped and checked her.

"It can't be overstated that I admire your loyalty, but this stubborn streak of yours is kind of annoying." But cute, he thought. As long as she used it for good, and by that he meant being on his side. Somehow he had to get her there.

"Isn't it lucky that you're leaving Rust Creek Falls and won't have to deal with me any longer, Detective?"

"I'm not going anywhere until we clarify some things." Now he was getting frustrated. And everyone in the crowded bar was watching and listening to what they were saying. Probably taking notes for the gossip column. It didn't escape his notice that some of the spectators were pointing, whispering, and money was changing hands. If he didn't miss his guess, they were betting on the outcome of this standoff.

What Russ had to say should be said in private, and he knew just the place. He reached for her hand and said, "Come with me."

She pulled away. "I don't think so."

"Wrong answer." Russ scooped her into his arms.

Lani made a surprised little sound, but he ignored her and turned toward the door. A man on a mission. It must have shown on his face because the customers standing around the bar with drinks in their hands parted like the Red Sea. He moved to the screen door and someone opened it for him. Russ appreciated that, since his arms were full of wiggly woman.

"Let me go," she said angrily.

"No."

"This is humiliating. Obviously, you haven't finished making me a joke in this town, one that I can never live down."

"This isn't a joke to me. All I want is for you to listen to what I have to say." He turned left and carried her down

Sawmill Street, past the Rust Creek garage and gas station. "So I'm taking you somewhere you can't run away."

Apparently, she was getting a clue about what he had in mind because she asked, "Are you arresting me?"

"Yes."

"What for?"

"Failure to yield."

"Oh, please. Don't pretend you're not relieved that I turned you down." Her tone dripped sarcasm even as her arms sneaked around his neck.

"If I was relieved, would I be carrying you through town?" Their faces were inches apart. "I mean this in the nicest possible way, Lani, but you're not a feather."

"Well, excuse me for not losing five pounds on the off chance that you were going to trump up charges and arrest me again. If I'm so heavy, just put me down."

"Nope."

Russ carried her to the door of the sheriff's office, and Gage opened it. Thank God he was still there.

"Got a citizen's tip from the Ace in the Hole," he explained.

"Here's another one for you," Russ said. "Go home."

"Understood."

"Wait," Lani said. "This is false arrest."

Grinning from ear to ear, the sheriff let himself out and closed the door behind him.

Russ carried her through the office and stopped in front of the empty cell they'd occupied the last time she was here. He used one hand to slide the barred door open then walked inside as it shut and automatically locked with the two of them inside.

He set her on the bunk. "Now you're a captive audience."

Lani blinked up at him, and suddenly all the sass and spirit were gone. She looked uncertain and vulnerable. "I don't understand. Why would you do this? It will be all over town soon, if it's not already. People will think we're… That you and I are…"

She was his life, that's what she was. She'd been there for her brother, for her family. There was no doubt in his mind that she would do the same for anyone she loved, and he hoped with everything he had that she cared about him.

"I love you, Lani."

"Since when?" She sat up straight, folded her arms over her chest and refused to look at him.

"Since the first time I saw you."

Her gaze jerked to his. "What?"

"I walked into the Ace in the Hole after working a shift for Gage. You were carrying a heavy tray full of beers, and I wondered how you didn't drop it. Surely the power of the lightning that hit me would knock you off balance."

"But you barely said a word to me." Her eyes were wide and so beautiful a man could drown in them and go down smiling.

"I couldn't. I knew if I did, resistance would be futile." He shrugged. "And I was right."

He looked around the cell, remembering the night he'd arrested her, in that wet yellow sundress that was practically transparent. It hadn't taken long for her to break him down, annihilate his defenses. He'd kissed her and was lost. The rest was history.

He sighed. "Even after the night you deliberately locked me in here and I fought against trusting you, I tried to ignore what I felt. My history had been nothing but a horrible warning."

"You and me both," she said.

"My instincts were telling me that you were exactly what you seemed—beautiful, loyal, someone who put her family first. Everything I ever wanted. But I couldn't trust that. My judgment was so far off I didn't have any faith in what my gut was telling me."

"What changed your mind?" There was the tiniest bit of skepticism in her voice.

"Two things." He blew out a breath. "When I faced the reality of leaving town and not seeing you every day, it felt wrong, empty. I've gotten used to seeing that pretty face, and leaving you was the last thing I wanted to do."

"What was the other thing?"

"Anderson told me about his legal battle and said that's why you deliberately got my attention the night he hit Skip Webster. That he couldn't afford to be arrested. And how he made you promise not to tell anyone."

"I can't believe he did that."

"Just so you know, he swore me to secrecy, too. And I plan to honor that promise just like you have. You set a high bar, Miss Dalton."

A small smile curved up the corners of her mouth. "So at the bar, Anderson was playing matchmaker."

"Yeah. And he's not the only one." At her questioning gaze he said, "Gage was at the sheriff's office when Anderson came in. After your brother left, he suggested I go to the Ace in the Hole and talk to you."

She smiled mysteriously.

"What's so funny?"

"I'm just trying to picture the two of them dressed as Cupid—tights, wings, the whole nine yards. Oh, wait. Cupid wears a diaper. Either way, not pretty," she said.

"Yeah." He dragged his fingers through his hair. "So, in front of everyone tonight, you defended my honor and said you love me."

"Yup, everyone heard," she agreed.

"Then there's only one thing left to do to close this

case." He moved in front of her and went down on one knee. "Marry me."

"Yes!" She grinned then threw herself into his arms and said, "I give myself up."

Epilogue

Lani snuggled up to Russ in the big king-size bed at his house in Boulder Junction. After the night he'd proposed in the jail cell, she'd all but moved in with him. He was back to work as a detective for Kalispell PD, working a shift for Gage now and then when he had time, to keep up the investigation into the wedding punch situation.

Every night after work they ended up in the bedroom, and sometimes they even watched TV. It turned out both of them liked crime dramas and trying to figure out whodunit. She took great pride in the fact that she guessed right as often as he did.

She fluffed the big pillows behind her then moved back in beside his big, warm body. He pulled her closer, and she rested her cheek on his chest, listening to the steady beat of his heart. He didn't know it yet but she had big plans to get that Kalispell PD T-shirt off him. Not that she didn't love the way it hugged all his delicious muscles, but she'd rather see and touch his bare skin.

Right now she was going to be smug and superior and rub in the fact that in the show they'd just finished watching, he had deduced wrong. "I told you it was the angry coworker."

He made a scoffing sound. "That was way too obvious. I was sure it was the nauseatingly sweet employer of the undocumented workers."

"You underestimate my investigative skills and powers of observation."

When he laughed, the sound vibrated through her. "I have never underestimated any of your powers, brainy Lani. Especially the power you have over me. You are one smart lady."

"Not smart enough to figure out who spiked that punch at the wedding."

"Yeah. It really bugs me that we couldn't solve the case." He shook his head. "All the shenanigans that went on that night, and no one saw anything."

Lani tapped her lip. "That's not entirely true, Russ. Whoever writes the gossip in Rust Creek Ramblings for the paper saw quite a bit. There were stories for weeks."

"Never could get an ID on the writer, either," he grumbled. "But I have an idea."

"Is it necessary to remind you that you're not on the case anymore?"

"Not full-time. But Gage asks me to follow up every once in a while. Besides, I can't stop thinking about it." He shrugged. "Occupational hazard."

"So what's your idea?" she asked.

"I think I'll send a note to the paper addressed to this anonymous columnist and ask whoever it is to come up with his or her own theory about the mystery. I think that will be irresistible to this person and could stir the waters. Maybe flush out the perp."

"It's worth a shot." She leaned back a little and looked

up at him. "You know that at some point you might have to put this in the unsolved file?"

"Yeah, but I hope not." There was an amazingly tender expression in his eyes when he looked at her. "And it's not about justice."

"Really?"

"Do you remember when we talked to Jordyn Leigh Clifton? When she said that she and Will are grateful for what happened. If they hadn't unknowingly gotten drunk that night and married, happiness might have passed them by."

"Yeah," she said. "Now I know what she meant. If that punch hadn't been spiked, my brothers wouldn't have mixed it up, and I wouldn't have danced in the fountain to save Anderson."

"And I wouldn't have arrested you."

She grinned happily. "Getting arrested wasn't nearly as bad as I thought. Both times it was kind of amazing, each in its own way."

"Yeah. As weird as it sounds, I'd really like to thank whoever messed with the punch at that wedding."

"I know what you mean." That day would always have a special place in her heart. "But I have to say when we get married, I'm a no vote on having an open punch bowl. I don't want my groom to be in detective mode on our big day."

"Where's your sense of adventure?" he teased.

"Alive and well." She caught the corner of her bottom lip between her teeth then decided to share something she'd been thinking about. "I really liked working the mystery with you. We make a good team.

"No argument there." He ran his finger along the side of her neck, over her chest, and stopped at the swell of her breast. "What's going on in that creative mind of yours?"

"This might sound a little crazy, but..." *Just spit it out.*

"We could open a detective agency, be like those husband-and-wife private investigators on TV."

"Hmm." His mouth was on her neck, and the single syllable vibrated through her.

"I have another idea." She reached for the bottom of his shirt. "Let's get this off."

"I'm a yes vote on that." His look was wicked as he whipped it off over his head then tossed it away. When he stared into her eyes, his expression was completely serious. "I love you, Lani."

"I know." There wasn't a doubt in her mind. "And I love you."

He wrapped her in his arms, and they were lost in each other for a long time. She was grateful for everything that happened. The park. The punch. A mystery ingredient. All of it had brought her to this moment and a lifetime of magic with her very own maverick.

* * * * *

Look for the next installment of the new Harlequin Special Edition continuity

MONTANA MAVERICKS:
WHAT HAPPENED AT THE WEDDING?

After a raucous July Fourth poker game, Brad Crawford finds himself in possession of the old Sullivan ranch, not realizing his "prize" also comes with a beautiful tenant—the former owner's daughter, Margot—who is determined to preserve her legacy. And her heart...

Don't miss

BETTING ON THE MAVERICK

by Cindy Kirk

On sale October 2015, wherever Harlequin books and ebooks are sold.

From New York Times *bestselling author*
Jodi Thomas comes a sweeping new series
set in a remote west Texas town—where
family can be made by blood or by choice...

RANSOM CANYON

Staten

WHEN HER OLD hall clock chimed eleven times, Staten Kirkland left Quinn O'Grady's bed. While she slept, he dressed in the shadows, watching her with only the light of the full moon. She'd given him what he needed tonight, and, as always, he felt as if he'd given her nothing.

Walking out to her porch, he studied the newly washed earth, thinking of how empty his life was except for these few hours he shared with Quinn. He'd never love her or anyone, but he wished he could do something for her. Thanks to hard work and inherited land, he was a rich man. She was making a go of her farm, but barely. He could help her if she'd let him. But he knew she'd never let him.

As he pulled on his boots, he thought of a dozen things he could do around the place. Like fixing that old tractor out in the mud or modernizing her irrigation system. The tractor had been sitting out by the road for months. If she'd accept his help, it wouldn't take him an hour to pull the old John Deere out and get the engine running again.

Only, she wouldn't accept anything from him. He knew better than to ask.

He wasn't even sure they were friends some days. Maybe they were more. Maybe less. He looked down at his palm, remembering how she'd rubbed cream on it and worried that all they had in common was loss and the need, now and then, to touch another human being.

The screen door creaked. He turned as Quinn, wrapped in an old quilt, moved out into the night.

"I didn't mean to wake you," he said as she tiptoed across the snow-dusted porch. "I need to get back. Got eighty new yearlings coming in early." He never apologized for leaving, and he wasn't now. He was simply stating facts. With the cattle rustling going on and his plan to enlarge his herd, he might have to hire more men. As always, he felt as though he needed to be on his land and on alert.

She nodded and moved to stand in front of him.

Staten waited. They never touched after they made love. He usually left without a word, but tonight she obviously had something she wanted to say.

Another thing he probably did wrong, he thought. He never complimented her, never kissed her on the mouth, never said any words after he touched her. If she didn't make little sounds of pleasure now and then, he wouldn't have been sure he satisfied her.

Now, standing so close to her, he felt more a stranger than a lover. He knew the smell of her skin, but he had no idea what she was thinking most of the time. She knew quilting and how to make soap from her lavender. She played the piano like an angel and didn't even own a TV. He knew ranching and watched from his recliner every game the Dallas Cowboys played.

If they ever spent over an hour talking they'd probably figure out they had nothing in common. He'd played every sport in high school, and she'd played in both the orchestra and the band. He'd collected most of his college hours online, and she'd gone all the way to New York to school. But, they'd loved the same person. Amalah had been Quinn's best friend and his one love. Only, they rarely talked about how they felt. Not anymore. Not ever really. It was too painful, he guessed, for both of them.

Tonight the air was so still, moisture hung like invisible lace. She looked to be closer to her twenties than her forties. Quinn had her own quiet kind of beauty. She always had, and he guessed she still would even when she was old.

To his surprise, she leaned in and kissed his mouth.

He watched her. "You want more?" he finally asked, figuring it was probably the dumbest thing to say to a naked woman standing two inches away from him. He had no idea what *more* would be. They always had sex once, if they had it at all, when he knocked on her door. Sometimes neither made the first move, and they just cuddled on the couch and held each other. Quinn wasn't a passionate woman. What they did was just satisfying a need that they both had now and then.

She kissed him again without saying a word. When her cheek brushed against his stubbled chin, it was wet and tasted newborn like the rain.

Slowly, Staten moved his hands under her blanket and circled her warm body, then he pulled her closer and kissed her fully like he hadn't kissed a woman since his wife died.

Her lips were soft and inviting. When he opened her mouth and invaded, it felt far more intimate than anything they had ever done, but he didn't stop. She wanted this from him, and he had no intention of denying her. No one would ever know that she was the thread that kept him together some days.

When he finally broke the kiss, Quinn was out of breath. She pressed her forehead against his jaw and he waited.

"From now on," she whispered so low he felt her words more than heard them, "when you come to see me, I need you to kiss me goodbye before you go. If I'm asleep, wake me. You don't have to say a word, but you have to kiss me."

She'd never asked him for anything. He had no intention of saying no. His hand spread across the small of her back and pulled her hard against him. "I won't forget if that's what you want." He could feel her heart pounding and knew her asking had not come easy.

She nodded. "It's what I want."

He brushed his lips over hers, loving the way she sighed as if wanting more before she pulled away.

"Good night," she said as though rationing pleasure. Stepping inside, she closed the screen door between them.

Raking his hair back, he put on his hat as he watched her fade into the shadows. The need to return was already building in him. "I'll be back Friday night if it's all right. It'll be late, I've got to visit with my grandmother and do her list of chores before I'll be free. If you like, I could bring barbecue for supper?" He felt as if he was rambling, but something needed to be said, and he had no idea what.

"And vegetables," she suggested.

He nodded. She wanted a meal, not just the meat. "I'll have them toss in sweet potato fries and okra."

She held the blanket tight as if he might see her body. She didn't meet his eyes when he added, "I enjoyed kissing you, Quinn. I look forward to doing so again."

With her head down, she nodded as she vanished into the darkness without a word.

He walked off the porch, deciding if he lived to be a hundred he'd never understand Quinn. As far as he knew, she'd never had a boyfriend when they were in school. And his wife had never told him about Quinn dating anyone special when she went to New York to that fancy music school. Now, in her forties, she'd never had a date, much less a lover that he knew of. But she hadn't been a virgin when they'd made love the first time.

Asking her about her love life seemed far too personal a question.

Climbing in his truck he forced his thoughts toward problems at the ranch. He needed to hire men; they'd lost three cattle to rustlers this month. As he planned the coming day, Staten did what he always did: he pushed Quinn to a corner of his mind, where she'd wait until he saw her again.

As he passed through the little town of Crossroads, all the businesses were closed up tight except for a gas station that stayed open twenty-four hours to handle the few travelers needing to refuel or brave enough to sample their food.

A quarter mile past the one main street of Crossroads, his truck lights flashed across four teenagers walking along the road between the Catholic church and the gas station.

Three boys and a girl. Fifteen or sixteen, Staten guessed.

For a moment the memory of Randall came to mind. He'd been about their age when he'd crashed, and he'd worn the same type of blue-and-white letter jacket that two of the boys wore tonight.

Staten slowed as he passed them. "You kids need a ride?" The lights were still on at the church, and a few cars were in the parking lot. Saturday night, Staten remembered. Members of 4-H would probably be working in the basement on projects.

One kid waved. A tall Hispanic boy named Lucas whom he thought was the oldest son of the head wrangler on the

Collins Ranch. Reyes was his last name, and Staten remembered the boy being one of a dozen young kids who were often hired part-time at the ranch.

Staten had heard the kid was almost as good a wrangler as his father. The magic of working with horses must have been passed down from father to son, along with the height. Young Reyes might be lean but, thanks to working, he would be in better shape than either of the football boys. When Lucas Reyes finished high school, he'd have no trouble hiring on at any of the big ranches, including the Double K.

"No, we're fine, Mr. Kirkland," the Reyes boy said politely. "We're just walking down to the station for a Coke. Reid Collins's brother is picking us up soon."

"No crime in that, mister," a redheaded kid in a letter jacket answered. His words came fast and clipped, reminding Staten of how his son had sounded.

Volume from a boy trying to prove he was a man, Staten thought.

He couldn't see the faces of the two boys with letter jackets, but the girl kept her head up. "We've been working on a project for the fair," she answered politely. "I'm Lauren Brigman, Mr. Kirkland."

Staten nodded. *Sheriff Brigman's daughter, I remember you.* She knew enough to be polite, but it was none of his business. "Good evening, Lauren," he said. "Nice to see you again. Good luck with the project."

When he pulled away, he shook his head. Normally, he wouldn't have bothered to stop. At this rate he'd turn into a nosy old man by forty-five. It didn't seem that long ago that he and Amalah used to walk up to the gas station after meetings at the church.

Hell, maybe Quinn asking to kiss him had rattled him more than he'd thought. He needed to get his head straight. She was just a friend. A woman he turned to when the storms came. Nothing more. That was the way they both wanted it.

Until he made it back to her porch next Friday night, he had a truckload of trouble at the ranch to worry about.

Lauren

A MIDNIGHT MOON blinked its way between storm clouds as Lauren Brigman cleaned the mud off her shoes. The guys had gone inside the gas station for Cokes. She didn't really want anything to drink, but it was either walk over with the others after working on their fair projects or stay back at the church and talk to Mrs. Patterson.

Somewhere Mrs. Patterson had gotten the idea that since Lauren didn't have a mother around, she should take every opportunity to have a "girl talk" with the sheriff's daughter.

Lauren wanted to tell the old woman that she had known all the facts of life by the age of seven, and she really did not need a buddy to share her teenage years with.

Reid Collins walked out from the gas station first with a can of Coke in each hand. "I bought you one even though you said you didn't want anything to drink," he announced as he neared. "Want to lean on me while you clean your shoes?"

Lauren rolled her eyes. Since he'd grown a few inches and started working out, Reid thought he was God's gift to girls.

"Why?" she asked as she tossed the stick. "I have a brick wall to lean on. And don't get any ideas we're on a date, Reid, just because I walked over here with you."

"I don't date sophomores," he snapped. "I'm on first string, you know. I could probably date any senior I want to. Besides, you're like a little sister, Lauren. We've known each other since you were in the first grade."

She thought of mentioning that playing first string on a football team that only had forty players total, including the coaches and water boy, wasn't any great accomplishment, but arguing with Reid would rot her brain. He'd been born rich, and he'd thought he knew everything since he'd cleared the birth canal. She feared his disease was terminal.

"If you're cold, I'll let you wear my football jacket." When she didn't comment, he bragged, "I had to reorder a bigger size after a month of working out."

She hated to, but if she didn't compliment him soon, he'd never stop begging. "You look great in the jacket, Reid. Half the seniors on the team aren't as big as you." There was nothing wrong with Reid from the neck down. In a few years he'd be a knockout with the Collins good looks and trademark rusty hair, not quite brown, not quite red. But he still wouldn't interest her.

"So, when I get my driver's license next month, do you want to take a ride?"

Lauren laughed. "You've been asking that since I was in the third grade and you got your first bike. The answer is still no. We're friends, Reid. We'll always be friends, I'm guessing."

He smiled a smile that looked as if he'd been practicing. "I know, Lauren, but I keep wanting to give you a chance now and then. You know, some guys don't want to date the sheriff's daughter, and I hate to point it out, babe, but if you don't fill out some, it's going to be bad news in college." He had the nerve to point at her chest. "From the looks of it, I seem to be the only one he'll let stand beside you, and that's just because our dads are friends."

She grinned. Reid was spoiled and conceited and self-centered, but she was right, they'd probably always be friends. Her dad was the sheriff, and his was the mayor of

Crossroads, even though he lived five miles from town on one of the first ranches established near Ransom Canyon.

Tim O'Grady, Reid's eternal shadow, walked out of the station with a huge frozen drink. The clear cup showed off its red-and-yellow layers of cherry-and-pineapple-flavored sugar.

Where Reid was balanced in his build, Tim was lanky, disjointed. He seemed to be made of mismatched parts. His arms were too long. His feet seemed too big, and his wired smile barely fit in his mouth. When he took a deep draw on his drink, he staggered and held his forehead from the brain freeze.

Lucas Reyes was the last of their small group to come outside. Lucas hadn't bought anything, but he evidently was avoiding standing with her. She'd known Lucas Reyes for a few years, maybe longer, but he never talked to her. Like Reid and Tim, he was a year ahead of her, but since he rarely talked, she usually only noticed him as a background person in her world.

Unlike them, Lucas didn't have a family name following him around opening doors for a hundred miles.

Reid repeated the plan. "My brother said he'd drop Sharon off and be back for us. But if they get busy doing their thing it could be an hour. We might as well walk back and sit on the church steps."

"We could start walking toward home," Lauren suggested as she pulled a tiny flashlight from her key chain. The canyon lake wasn't more than a mile. If they walked they wouldn't be so cold. She could probably be home before Reid's dumb brother could get his lips off Sharon. If rumors were true, Sharon had very kissable lips, among other body parts.

"Better than standing around here," Reid said as Tim kicked mud toward the building. "I'd rather be walking than sitting. Plus, if we go back to the church, Mrs. Patterson will probably come out to keep us company."

Without a vote, they started walking.

Within a few yards, Reid and Tim had fallen behind and were lighting up a smoke. To her surprise, Lucas stayed beside her.

"You don't smoke?" she asked, not really expecting him to answer.

"No, can't afford the habit," he said, surprising her. "I've got plans, and they don't include lung cancer."

Maybe the dark night made it easier to talk, or maybe Lauren didn't want to feel so alone in the shadows. "I was starting to think you were a mute. We've had a few classes together, and you've never said a word. Even tonight you were the only one who didn't talk about your project."

Lucas shrugged. "Didn't see the point. I'm just entering for the prize money, not trying to save the world or build a better tomorrow."

"Hey, you two deadbeats up there!" Reid yelled. "I got an idea."

Lauren didn't want the conversation with Lucas to end, but if she ignored Reid he'd just get louder. "What?"

Reid ran up between them and put an arm over both her and Lucas's shoulders. "How about we break into the Gypsy House? I hear it's haunted by Gypsies who died a hundred years ago."

Tim caught up to them. As always, he agreed with Reid. "Look over there in the trees. The place is just waiting for us. Heard if you rattle a Gypsy's bones, the dead will speak to you." Tim's eyes glowed in the moonlight. "I had a cousin once who said he heard voices in that old place, and no one was there but him."

"This is not a good idea." Lauren tried to back away, but Reid held her shoulder tight.

"Come on, Lauren, for once in your life, do something

that's not safe. No one's lived in the old place for years. How much trouble can we get into?"

"It's just a rotting old house," Lucas said so low no one heard but Lauren. "There's probably rats or rotten floors. It's an accident waiting to happen. How about you come back in the daylight, Reid, if you really want to explore the place?"

"We're all going, now," Reid announced as he shoved Lauren off the road and into the trees that blocked the view of the old homestead from passing cars. "Think of the story we'll have to tell everyone Monday. We will have explored a haunted house and lived to tell the tale."

Reason told her to protest more strongly, but at fifteen, reason wasn't as intense as the possibility of an adventure. Just once, she'd have a story to tell. Just this once...her father wouldn't find out.

They rattled across the rotting porch steps fighting tumbleweeds that stood like flimsy guards around the place. The door was locked and boarded up. The smell of decay hung in the foggy air, and a tree branch scraped against one side of the house as if whispering for them to stay back.

The old place didn't look like much. It might have been the remains of an early settlement, built solid to face the winters with no style or charm. Odds were, Gypsies never even lived in it. It appeared to be a half dugout with a second floor built on years later. The first floor was planted down into the earth a few feet, so the second floor windows were just above their heads, giving the place the look of a house that had been stepped on by a giant.

Everyone called it the Gypsy House because a group of hippies had squatted there in the Seventies. No one remembered when the hippies had moved on, or who owned the house now, but somewhere in its past a family named Stanley must have lived there because old-timers called it the Stanley house.

"I heard devil worshippers lived here years ago." Tim began making scary movie soundtrack noises. "Body parts are probably scattered in the basement. They say once Satan moves in, only the blood of a virgin will wash the place clean."

Reid's laughter sounded nervous. "That leaves me out."

Tim jabbed his friend. "You wish. I say you'll be the first to scream."

"Shut up, Tim." Reid's uneasy voice echoed in the night. "You're freaking me out. Besides, there is no basement. It's just a half dugout built into the ground, so we'll find no buried bodies."

Lauren screamed as Reid kicked a low window in, and all the guys laughed.

"You go first, Lucas," Reid ordered. "I'll stand guard."

To Lauren's surprise, Lucas slipped into the space. His feet hit the ground with a thud somewhere in the blackness.

"You next, Tim," Reid announced as if he were the commander.

"Nope. I'll go after you." All Tim's laughter had disappeared. Apparently he'd frightened himself.

"I'll go." Lauren suddenly wanted this entire adventure to be over with. With her luck, animals were wintering in the old place.

"I'll help you down." Reid lowered her into the window space.

As she moved through total darkness, her feet wouldn't quite touch the bottom. For a moment she just hung, afraid to tell Reid to drop her.

Then, she felt Lucas's hands at her waist. Slowly he took her weight.

"I'm in," she called back to Reid. He let her hands go, and she dropped against Lucas.

"You all right?" Lucas whispered near her hair.

"This was a dumb idea."

She could feel him breathing as Reid finally landed, cussing the darkness. For a moment it seemed all right for Lucas to stay close; then in a blink, he was gone from her side.

Now the tiny flashlight offered Lauren some much-needed light. The house was empty except for an old wire bed frame and a few broken stools. With Reid in the lead, they moved up rickety stairs to the second floor, where shadowy light came from big dirty windows.

Tim hesitated when the floorboards began to rock as if the entire second story were on some kind of seesaw. He backed down the steps a few feet, letting the others go first. "I don't know if this second story will hold us all." Fear rattled in his voice.

Reid laughed and teased Tim as he stomped across the second floor, making the entire room buck and pitch. "Come on up, Tim. This place is better than a fun house."

Stepping hesitantly on the upstairs floor, Lauren felt Lucas just behind her and knew he was watching over her.

Tim dropped down a few more steps, not wanting to even try.

Lucas backed against the wall between the windows, his hand still brushing Lauren's waist to keep her steady as Reid jumped to make the floor shake. The whole house seemed to moan in pain, like a hundred-year-old man standing up one arthritic joint at a time.

When Reid yelled for Tim to join them, Tim started back up the broken stairs, just before the second floor buckled and crumbled. Tim dropped out of sight as rotten lumber pinned him halfway between floors.

His scream of pain ended Reid's laughter.

In a blink, dust and boards flew as pieces of the roof rained down on them and the second floor vanished below them, board by rotting board.

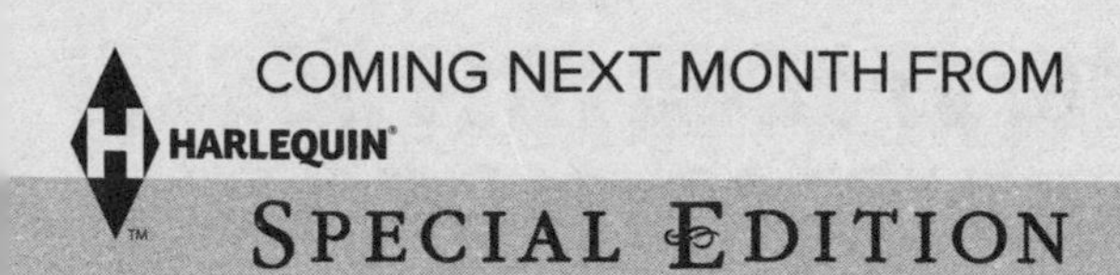

Available September 15, 2015

#2431 THE GOOD GIRL'S SECOND CHANCE

The Bravos of Justice Creek • by Christine Rimmer

Single dad Quinn Bravo and Chloe Winchester plan to spend only one night together. But the former bad boy finds he can't get the beautiful blonde out of his system that easily. Factor in his little girl, who desperately wants a mommy, and he's got the recipe for a perfect instant family!

#2432 BETTING ON THE MAVERICK

Montana Mavericks: What Happened at the Wedding?
by Cindy Kirk

When Brad Crawford wins a neighbor's ranch in a poker game, the cowboy gets more than he'd ever bargained for. Former rodeo rider Margot Sullivan, a feisty rancher's daughter, is determined to preserve her family's legacy. But what happens when love gets in the way?

#2433 ROCK-A-BYE BRIDE

The Colorado Fosters • by Tracy Madison

Anna Rockwood hadn't expected a fling with Logan Daugherty to result in a pregnancy, let alone a marriage! *She* wants real love, while *he* insists on doing the "honorable thing." But their hopes and dreams collide when they form the family of a lifetime.

#2434 THE BOSS'S MARRIAGE PLAN

Proposals & Promises • by Gina Wilkins

Scott Prince proposes marriage to his office manager, Tess Miller. He's ready to stop his family's insistent queries about his love life. Their future seems bright, but when they both develop real feelings for one another, can the bachelor find happily-ever-after with his true love?

#2435 THE TYCOON'S PROPOSAL

The Barlow Brothers • by Shirley Jump

Workaholic CEO Mac Barlow wants Savannah Hillstrand's company—and she *really* needs his business acumen. So she proposes a plan that will cater to both their interests. But what Savannah doesn't count on is the warm heart buried deep in Mac's brawny chest, or the love that will blossom in her own...

#2436 THE PUPPY PROPOSAL

Paradise Animal Clinic • by Katie Meyer

After a traumatic childhood, vet tech Jillian Everett has finally found a home in Paradise Isle, Florida. But when hotelier Nic Caruso threatens to destroy her community, Jillian is determined not to let him. So what if he's sexy *and* helps her rescue adorable dogs? That doesn't mean he's The One...or does it?

YOU CAN FIND MORE INFORMATION ON UPCOMING HARLEQUIN® TITLES, FREE EXCERPTS AND MORE AT WWW.HARLEQUIN.COM.

HSECNM0915